# HONEY & PEPPER

*When in Pheme Book 1*

## A.J. DEMAS

**Honey & Pepper**

A.J. Demas



Cover art by Vic Gray
Cover design by Alice Degan

# CHAPTER 1

Nikias had a fresh batch of octopus fritters ready when the three bells rang out from the harbour. He turned them out of the pan onto a dish, drizzled them with sauce, and slid the dish onto the front counter of the snack stand, pleased with his timing.

It wasn't good business sense, making a fresh batch of their most expensive item at three bells, which was long before quitting time for the dock hands who would come pouring up the Shipyard Road on their way home from the harbour and made up most of the snack stand's customers. Widow Pyke, the owner of the snack stand and Nikias's boss, wouldn't have approved of it if she had known, but he was minding the stand by himself that afternoon, during the slow period. And three bells was the hour when, often, the law clerk emerged from the door of the house beside Pyke's Snacks, and, if he wasn't in a hurry, stopped at the counter and ordered something. Usually octopus fritters.

Once, when Nikias happened to have turned out a fresh batch just as the clerk emerged—he had been later than usual that day—he commented appreciatively on their freshness. "They melt in your mouth," was what he'd said. Since then,

Nikias had been waiting for an opportunity to have a fresh batch ready when he thought the clerk might come by.

He didn't know the man's name. In fact, it was only a guess that he was a law clerk—he might be something else, but Nikias had often seen him carrying scrolls with official-looking red ribbons and seals dangling from them. He did some kind of work, anyway, for the Photionis family, who owned the house and the little corner property that Widow Pyke rented for her snack stand.

Nikias leaned on the counter, idly rearranging the plates of stuffed dates and cheese pastries to show off the fresh octopus fritters. He heard the house door opening, but knew immediately it wasn't the law clerk. It was someone being thrown out of the house; Nikias could hear his raised voice as soon as the door opened.

He had seen this happen two or three times before, in the half-year since he began working at the snack stand. What-ever business the Photionis family did—and he gathered they did some kind of business—they made some of their clients spitting mad. They had a big, broad-shouldered slab of a doorman who was more than up to the task of throwing these people out and shutting the door firmly behind them.

Today's client was the worst that Nikias had seen yet. He was clawing at the doorman's face as he was pushed backward over the threshold, shrieking abuse.

"You'll suck Nepharos's dick in hell, you pirates! You goat-buggerers! We had a *contract*, you—"

He left off with a squawk when the doorman shoved him hard enough to make him stumble. But it wasn't enough to silence him for long. He wasn't a giant like the doorman, but he was big enough. He gathered breath to spew more blas-phemy as he scrabbled in his clothes for something.

Nikias found himself swinging around the counter into the street before he even saw the flash of metal in the man's hand. The doorman was halfway back through the house door, but the client wasn't going for him. He was lunging out into the street, aiming for another figure strolling toward the house. The client caught the newcomer by surprise, twisting his arm behind his back, the knife blade flashing up to his throat. Nikias, out in the street now but still too far away, stood helpless as the red-ribboned scrolls dropped and bounced on the cobbles.

The clerk stood frozen in the big man's grip, as if—the idea flashed into Nikias's mind—he had been in similar situations before and knew it would be useless to struggle. He was a much slighter man, though as tall as his attacker. Nothing about him suggested he knew how to fight. His brand-new blue cloak and tunic had been tugged awry when the man grabbed him, exposing a triangle of white skin and smooth collarbone. The knife's edge had drawn a tiny line of blood on the side of his throat.

"What is it you want, Demokritos?" The clerk spoke first, his voice level and calm.

"What do I want?" the client growled. "I want what's written in my contract—the contract you wrote with your own hand, you little shit. I want what's owed me."

"I see. If you had read the contract, I'm sure you would notice that Hesteus and his heirs were free to cancel it."

"Nepharos's nine hells they were! Old Photis never would have left me out in the cold, and neither will his sons. We're going in there to talk to that spineless goat-fucker again." Demokritos gave his prisoner a shove toward the doorway.

Nikias saw the young man wince as he was wrenched around, and then, so quickly he had barely time to register it, the clerk shoved back against his captor and twisted lithely away from his knife. The knife dropped to the stones of the street, the doorman lunged forward, and the client bolted. The clerk and the doorman let him go, both of them looking after him, clearly not intending to give chase.

Nikias had remained standing uselessly in the street

through the whole thing. He came forward now and knelt to gather up the clerk's scrolls. The doorman was asking if the clerk was all right. He had dropped briefly to his knees, but he was up again, holding a handkerchief to the scratch on his neck, waving the doorman away.

"I'm fine."

The doorman looked sceptical. "That was some quick thinking. Quick acting, too. Very impressive."

The clerk gave a soft snort. "Thanks. I got good training around here, before your time. Tell the master I'll be in—actually, no. Don't tell him I'm here yet, will you."

"No trouble. Take your time."

The doorman turned back into the house, and the clerk looked at Nikias, still standing there with the scrolls in his hands.

"That must have been alarming for you," the clerk said, almost brightly.

"Sir," said Nikias. He held out the scrolls.

"Thanks. I don't suppose you've got any octopus fritters today?"

"Of course, sir."

After a moment more of standing there like an idiot, Nikias turned and headed back to the snack stand. The clerk strolled after him.

"They're—um—fresh," Nikias stammered as he got behind the counter.

"Wonderful. They're best fresh, aren't they?"

Nikias had to concentrate to keep his hands from shaking too badly as he threaded the fritters onto a skewer and set the whole thing in a dish. He looked up to see his customer counting out coins onto the counter. His hands were shaking too, and his face was a dead white.

"Don't worry about change," he said, setting down the last coin.

"Sir," said Nikias, "there's a stool back here. Would you like to sit down?"

The clerk hesitated a moment, then came around the end of the counter, where Nikias was pointing, and perched gingerly on the stool in the cramped interior of the snack stand.

"Thanks," he said, his voice subdued.

Nikias handed him the dish with the skewer of octopus fritters and turned to scoop the coins off the counter and drop them into the cash box.

"If you want more sauce," he said, almost in a whisper, "the jar's right behind you."

"Oh," said the other, in the same tone. "Extra sauce. That's special."

When Nikias turned around, he had set down his scrolls on the counter and was delicately pulling a fritter off the skewer with his teeth. He always ate them that way. Some people pulled them off with their fingers, and some people chewed them off messily, but he ate tidily and carefully, like a cat.

Nikias pulled out the other stool, which had been tucked under the far counter, and sat on it. The interior of the snack stand was barely big enough for two men. Widow Pyke was very small, and even she complained about how much space Nikias took up. He realized he had never been this close to the clerk before, or not without the snack-stand counter between them, which made a difference.

He remembered the first time he had seen the clerk, which had also been his first day working at Pyke's Snacks. He didn't remember what he had been doing before that, or what happened after, just the feeling of his heart twisting in his chest like a wrung-out rag because the law clerk—whom he hadn't thought of as "the law clerk" then—was the most beautiful man he'd ever seen.

He had the kind of slender, sinuous body that did everything gracefully—standing, walking, leaning, gesturing, everything—and his skin was peachy pale. His eyes were a warm, surprising light brown that flashed up at you from beneath very long lashes, and his black hair had a wave to it that was not quite curls. He wore it in a careless style, almost long enough to brush his shoulders. There was something unreal about his colouring, the subtle contrasts of it, something impossibly delicate.

Nikias watched the clerk's hands holding the skewer of fried octopus, memorizing their beauty of movement, the proportions of his long fingers, the play of light and shadow on the knuckles and the tendons that moved under the white skin.

"You're usually leaving at the three bells," he found himself saying, randomly. "Not coming back."

The light brown eyes snapped up, wide and wary. Nikias realized he had spoken as if he watched the clerk's movements carefully—because he did—and that this must sound sinister, especially to someone who wasn't entirely surprised to be held hostage outside his employer's door. The clerk must have a highly developed sense for danger.

"Sorry, sorry," Nikias gabbled out, before the other had a chance to say anything—if he had been going to say anything, and it seemed like he hadn't. "I don't mean anything by it. You're a regular customer. I just happened to notice … when you usually come."

The clerk looked away, turning on his stool to dip the ladle into the jar of sauce and drizzle some onto his remaining fritters, holding the skewer neatly over the dish.

"You make these yourself, don't you?"

"Those, yes. I'm often here by myself in the afternoons."

"So you are."

"So anything fresh, I make myself. The dates and pastries we do in the morning."

The clerk was silent for a moment, chewing. Nikias tried

not to look too pointedly at his mouth. His lips were mobile, cleanly shaped, exquisite.

"You do a better job of these than the old lady."

"Oh. Thank you." He almost started to explain that he used a different technique, didn't deep-fry them the way Pyke used to, but he realized that would be either very obvious or very boring, depending on how much the clerk cared.

"She's had this shop for decades," the clerk said. "Ever since I can remember. It used to be her and her husband, back when I was a boy. I think you're the first assistant she's hired since he died. Of course, you probably know all this."

"No," said Nikias, "I didn't."

It should have been interesting information, giving him a window onto his grumpy boss's past that helped him understand her better. If he was the first man to work alongside her in the snack stand since her husband, no wonder she complained about how much space he took up. It must have brought back memories that made her sad.

But he didn't want to be talking about Widow Pyke. He wanted to ask the clerk about himself. Was he all right after the attack? Would there be another? Why did he work for these people who had to employ a doorman big enough to throw knife-wielding clients into the street, anyway? And those things the man had said about his employer—were they true?

"So, you … " Nikias started. "You came here as a boy?"

"Mm, yes, often."

The clerk finished the last dripping fritter on his skewer and carefully wiped his mouth and fingers with his handkerchief. He got to his feet, smiling, and picked up his scrolls from the counter.

"Thank you," he said, moving around the front counter and back out into the sunlight of the street.

"Thank you, sir," said Nikias, on his feet now as well.

"You don't have to call me 'sir.' My name's Kallion."

"Kallion. Oh. I'm Nikias."

"Good to meet you, Nikias."

"I'll—I'll remember next time, si—Kallion. That you like extra sauce."

Kallion nodded coolly at the doorman as if nothing out of the ordinary had happened. Dolon nodded back in the same style, and Kallion strolled through into the house where he had lived until six months ago.

"Master's in the menagerie," Dolon called after him. "I'd wait for him to come out if I was you."

Kallion walked through the vast atrium, back through the rear corridors and out into the garden. He passed by the fountain with its gilded statue of a pudgy young god Soukos, playing in a disturbingly intimate way with a dolphin, and arrived at the gates of the fenced-off area at the back of the garden that housed the menagerie. From the nearby summer dining room, he could hear the mistress of the house, Rhoias, arguing—or maybe "pleading"was a better word—with her sister-in-law.

"But how will it look, Elpis? Having a party with my husband only six months dead? Wouldn't it be better not to have it this year?"

Elpis laughed. "Don't be a goose—no one thinks you cared for Hesteus. I've already invited all the usual people. We have to keep up the connections, you know, for the sake of the family business. And who knows? Perhaps you'll find a new husband among them."

Rhoias made an unhappy noise.

Kallion pushed open the gate to the menagerie. He always had to steel himself to step over the threshold, and he hated it.

*They won't hurt you*, was what Old Photis, who had the

menagerie built, always used to say to guests when he showed them around. That might have been true, or it might not, and Kallion had always, even as a boy, found it disingenuous, because surely the whole point of Old Photis's menagerie was that all the animals looked very much like they would hurt you—like they would eat you as an afternoon snack, given the chance, and it wouldn't spoil their appetite for dinner.

The current master of the house was feeding the crocodile when Kallion came in. Epaphras Photionis stood leaning gingerly on the stone wall around the crocodile's pond, cautiously flinging bits of meat from a dish beside him. One of his slaves, a thin boy named Chares, was holding the dish and looking sick with anxiety. Epaphras didn't look much happier.

The head of the Photionis family was a man of medium build, with closely clipped dark hair and a handsome, sad-eyed face. If he had smiled at all in the six months since he had inherited the house and everything that came with it, Kallion hadn't seen it.

"Kallion!" he cried. "Are you all right? Is it true you were attacked on the doorstep?"

"I'm fine, sir," said Kallion quickly. "I gather you cancelled Demokritos's contract?"

"Yes." Epaphras winced. "He wasn't very happy about that, but I had to. Since I sold the gaming houses, we've no more use for those coins, and … " He shrugged, a piece of meat dangling limply from his fingers. "I can't keep people on out of charity, can I?"

Kallion nodded mutely, because he wasn't going to answer that. Continuing to pay a forger to produce debased coins would be a strange form of charity.

Epaphras tossed the last piece of meat and made a motion as if to run his hands through his hair, then thought better of it. "How long do crocodiles live, Kallion? Any idea?"

"Er … quite a long time, I think, sir."

"Damnation. Do you want to press charges?"

"Against the … Oh. Against Demokritos. No." It honestly hadn't occurred to him that he could. A rather strange idea. "I don't think we want any of that in court."

"No. Obviously not. Well, if you're sure … " Epaphras looked like he was trying to conceal his relief.

"I thought I heard Elpis and Rhoias talking about a party when I came in," Kallion ventured.

"Yes, yes, for the Euthalion, as usual. It seems to mean a lot to Elpis." He shrugged.

Kallion opened his mouth to ask whether that was a good reason to have it, but then he closed it again. It had never been his place to ask such questions, and now it wasn't even something that concerned him.

"More contracts?" Epaphras said, gesturing at the scrolls Kallion was carrying.

"Yes, sir. These are the ones I brought home with me the other day. I have had a look through them, and I think there are some we may be able to settle."

"Good man," said Epaphras approvingly. They moved toward the gate, Chares following.

"I should warn you, sir," said Kallion. "Some of them are … pretty bad."

Epaphras winced. "Well, those are the ones that need our attention the most urgently, aren't they? I can't tell you how much I appreciate your help with all of this, Kallion. I know you must wish you could get on with your career and leave this place behind."

This was unanswerable, because of course it was true; Kallion would have given anything not to have set foot in Old Photis's house ever again. As they walked back out into the familiar garden, it struck him forcefully how true that was, how every paving stone, every gold-embellished column, even the scents of the flowers, stirred a feeling in the pit of his stomach that was some kind of mixture of hatred and fear.

"I would not have a career if not for you, sir," he said politely.

Epaphras laughed. "You surely would, but I am glad to have helped."

On his way out of the house, later, Kallion glanced at the snack stand where he had sat for a few minutes that morning. It was odd to think that today was the first time he'd ever been inside that little place, which had been owned by the same woman, serving the same greasy snacks, for as long as he could remember. Except that the snacks weren't exactly the same these days; the new assistant certainly did make better octopus fritters than his employer. Nikias—his name was Nikias.

He used a different technique, Kallion thought—didn't deep-fry them but cooked them in a pan or something. Kallion had been meaning to ask him about it, as an excuse to make conversation, because the other big improvement that Nikias brought to the snack stand was that he was impossibly cute.

He was still there when Kallion looked, alone, the counter empty of customers, but he was busy with something, his back turned to the street. Kallion's nerve deserted him, and he walked on past.

# CHAPTER 2

THE OPPORTUNITY NIKIAS had been waiting for came only three days later. So it was hardly fair to say he'd been waiting for it at all, but those three days had felt long. At home in his tiny fifth-floor room, lying awake on his bed listening to his downstairs neighbours fight or his next-door neighbours make love (awkwardly, from the sound of it), he had returned again and again to that scene in the street, wishing it could have gone differently. He saw himself, in his mind's eye, hauling Kallion's attacker back by the hair and flinging him down to the cobbles, or sweeping Kallion up into his arms in some sort of dramatic gesture that he actually had no idea how to execute.

When he had run out into the street that day, sensing that the desperate client was about to draw a knife, he'd known what he intended to do. He knew what he *would* have done, if he'd been closer. He wasn't incompetent. But he'd been too far away, too centrally in the man's line of sight. If he had moved closer, the man might have reacted, disastrously.

He didn't think he'd done the wrong thing, but it was still galling to think that Kallion had just seen him standing there like a post, doing nothing more useful than gathering up his scrolls after the danger was over and offering him extra sauce for his octopus fritters.

So he decided he would have to look for another opportunity. Not to rescue Kallion from a knife-wielding attacker, of course, because it would be better if that kind of situation never arose again. But he could be of some other use, make some other impression on Kallion.

The first step to doing that, he reasoned, was to get inside the Photionis house somehow, to find out what went on in there and how Kallion was involved. Lying awake for long chunks of three nights, Nikias turned over a number of unfeasible plans, discarding each with a weary practicality which did not quite desert him even in the depth of the night. And then, on the third day, the opportunity presented itself, almost spontaneously.

Kallion had not stopped by the snack stand in the days since, and in fact Nikias had only seen him once, hurrying into the house. But there were other members of the household who occasionally stopped at the stand, and one who sometimes stayed to make conversation.

Her name was Itia, and she was from the same island as Nikias. That was their only bond, but it was enough for her. She was a few years older than he and had many more memories of their homeland than he did, and she seemed to enjoy rehearsing them with someone who had at least breathed the same air at one time. Even Pyke, who had been inclined to tease Nikias gruffly about her at first, had eventually admitted that what she was doing was not flirting.

That morning, when Itia stopped by the snack stand, she didn't come to talk about Pyria but to complain about her household.

"They're having the Euthalion party this year after all." She shook her head wearily. "It's so much work, and now at the last minute, too. We all thought it wouldn't happen, with

Master Hesteus being, you know … ” She waved a hand to mean something, Nikias wasn't sure what.

“He's sick?” he suggested, leaning on the counter.

“He's dead,” said Pyke, banging down a dish of pastries. “And good—”

“Shh!” Itia cut her off sharply. “They think he's dead. They're pretty sure. The court's *said* that he's dead, declared it officially, so Master Epaphras could inherit and look after the house and things. But they never found his body. We'd all be happier if they'd found his body.” After a moment, as if she'd heard how that sounded, she added, “I mean we'd know for certain. Not knowing for certain, that's hard. That's all I meant.”

Nikias would have sworn she had really meant “happier.”

“Anyway, we all thought Master Epaphras would call off the Euthalion party this year—but he hasn't. Mistress Elpis has organized it all. She used to be in charge of it in Master Hesteus's day too.”

“The widow?” said Nikias, scandalized.

“No, the sister,” Pyke supplied.

“That's not much better! The house is in mourning, and they're having a Euthalion party?”

“It's been six months,” said Pyke. “And I'll bet my last obios nobody misses him.”

“Shh,” said Itia.

“It's a big party?” Nikias prompted, to change the subject slightly. “What's it like?”

Itia sighed. “In Master Hesteus's day, awful. I don't know if all the same people will show up now that he's gone. But I can thank Anaxe I'll be needed in the kitchen and won't have to serve the guests.”

Nikias gave the dough he was working another pass with the rolling pin. “Are they hiring for the night?” he asked casually.

He wished Pyke hadn't been in the stand to hear this. He

didn't want her to think that she didn't pay him enough and that was why he needed to look for extra work. But it couldn't be helped.

"They're hiring, yes," said Itia, "but you don't want to work for them."

"If they pay well, I might. Who do I talk to? Would you put in a word for me?"

He didn't care that he sounded rude and overeager. Anyone could imagine a plausible story for why he might need extra money—he could tell both Itia and Pyke one later, if they wanted to know—and paid work was hard to come by, everyone knew that.

"I don't know what she's paying, but it might have to be a lot. People wouldn't come back to work for her otherwise." Itia smiled faintly. "I'll talk to Cook for you. You just want to see what goes on, don't you? You boys are all the same."

After she left, Nikias was left with Pyke, who stood considering him with her arms folded across her chest.

"Is that it? You just want to see what goes on at a wild Photionis party? Or is there more to this? You don't need money for something particular, do you? Gambling debts? Get a girl in trouble?"

"No! No, Itia was right." Then, because Pyke had asked that as if she was genuinely concerned about him, and it reminded him a little of the woman who had raised him, he added honestly, "Well, partly. I want to find out what goes on in that house, in general."

"No, you don't. Trust me."

"Yes, you see—that's exactly why I do. All I get are vague mutters and dark looks. What are these people, anyway? Gangsters?"

"Shh-shh!" Pyke flapped her hands in a violent shushing motion, although he had spoken, if anything, in a low voice. "Of course they're gangsters! Why do you need to know any more than that?"

"Because … I don't know, because I've never met gangsters." Didn't even, if he was perfectly honest, know quite what the word meant—and he'd felt a kind of thrill down his spine when Pyke had confirmed that's what they were. "And they're our neighbours. Your landlords."

Pyke pursed her lips and looked at him assessingly for a moment. "Old Photis was my landlord, our landlord, when Tono and I first set up in this street, twenty-eight years ago. He was … a great man, in his way. And a bad man in most ways, if you take my meaning."

Nikias wasn't sure that he did, but he didn't interrupt.

"He'd built his business up from nothing, and some of it might not have been quite legal—most of it might not have been at all legal. But as a landlord, as a family man … he cared for people, you know. Took care of his own. Even his slaves—I don't expect he knew his letters himself, but he had all the children of his slaves trained up in one thing and another, painting and riding and oratory and that, and used to enter them in competitions to show them off."

Nikias made a face. That was not his idea of "caring for people." Pyke's gaze had turned reminiscent.

"He had three children of his own—Elpis, the daughter, is the eldest, Hesteus and Epaphras are much younger. They were babies when Tono and I first came, but I suppose even Epaphras must be thirty by now. Hesteus inherited in the year of the last big earthquake and took over the family business—in spite of what everyone said, his father *hadn't* written him out of the will. Of course … "

She fell suddenly silent, as if she had only just noticed that she had been telling a story about the past, including the name of her late husband, which in six months Nikias had never yet heard. And it sounded like she had been on the verge of saying something really interesting.

"Of course … *what?*" he prompted finally.

Pyke pursed her lips again, and Nikias began to wonder

seriously if he would be able to restrain himself from shaking her—which would be shocking, her a tiny old woman and him a great big young man.

"Well, they're both dead now. Photis and Hesteus, and only that fool Epaphras and that ghastly Elpis left. And as for the business … " She shrugged. "Customers coming, Nikias —get back to work."

Itia was as good as her word, and she came back that evening around closing time to tell Nikias that the cook would like to meet him. She waited, chatting about Pyria, while he began putting things away in the stand. Then he heard her say, "Oh, hello ma'am," in a tone of subdued surprise.

He stood up from where he had been stooping to put away the crock of flour, and saw an absolutely stunning woman standing in the street in front of the snack stand.

She was probably ten years older than Nikias, and she was almost his height, her plum-coloured mantle wrapped closely around her curves. Her hair was black and lavishly curly, her skin a dark, glowing olive, and she had the most extraordinarily beautiful eyebrows.

"Hello, Itia," she said, her voice melodious and warm.

Itia was still looking surprised, perhaps by the fact that the woman remembered her name, and she didn't appear to know what to say.

"I'm about to close up for the day, ma'am," said Nikias, coming to her rescue, "but can I get you anything? I've a batch of cheese fritters that are quite fresh. I was going to take them home for my own dinner, but I'd be delighted to sell them to you instead."

"Oh, you're so sweet," said the woman, approaching the counter and inspecting the cheese fritters. "Mm, they do look good. I'll take two—no, three."

As he was wrapping the fritters, she asked, "Did you take over from Widow Pyke? I see her name's still on the sign."

"Oh, it's still her business, ma'am. I work for her."

"Ah, do you? Lovely. She has been in the neighbourhood a long time. Oh, don't bother tying it—I am going to eat them right now, in the street, like a dockhand." She laughed gorgeously.

She paid for the fritters and did, indeed, stand in the street and eat them out of the wrapper, rather messily, and exclaimed over how good they were, while Nikias finished closing up the stall and Itia loitered looking uncomfortable.

"Well," the beautiful woman announced, when she had finished her fritters and wiped her fingers on her mantle, "those were better than anything I ever had from this stall in the old days. Pyke is lucky to have you, young man!"

Nikias, out of the stall and locking the shutters by this time, smiled and made modest noises.

"Well," said the woman again. She turned toward the door of the Photionis house, and did something that could only be described as squaring her shoulders, which Nikias did not think he had ever seen a woman do. "Time to face it, I suppose."

"Let's go," Itia hissed at Nikias.

He would have found some excuse to linger and see what happened when the woman knocked on the house door, but since Itia obviously wanted to get away, he followed her obediently. She led the way down a grimy slit of an alley along the far side of the house, where he had almost to walk sideways to pass through, to a gate opening onto a small and dismal kitchen yard.

"Who—" he started.

"Who was that woman?" she finished for him. "Master Epaphras's wife. Ex-wife? I'm not sure. She left him, oh, years ago, not long after Old Photis died and Master Hesteus became head of the family—in fact, I *think* that had something to do with it, I think she wanted Epaphras to stand up to his brother, and she left him because he wouldn't. And now she's back!"

Nikias whistled. "That's a piece of news. You'd better get inside and share it before everyone finds out from someone else."

She swatted at him, and he grinned.

They went inside, and while Itia made the rounds with her gossip, Nikias met the cook, and the steward, who, as it turned out, was in charge of hiring extra help for the party, and was annoyed that the cook had promised work to complete unknowns without telling him. He was mollified, though, by the sight of Nikias, who he said was presentable enough to serve outside the kitchen. Nikias said, truthfully, that that suited him well.

They needed more help outside the kitchen than in, the steward explained, because though the guests would want to eat, they would also want to drink, and a lot more of the latter than the former, and keeping up with the demand for wine, and the vagaries of the guests when they had had too much, would tax the regular household staff beyond their limit. From this Nikias concluded, with a slight thrill, that this was going to be the sort of party that he had heard about but never before served at. It was going to be a debauch.

The cook and the steward, like Itia, were slaves. It felt very odd to Nikias—even wrong—to discuss with these men a night's work for which he would be paid, and generously too. It had been less than a year since Nikias himself was freed. He was glad he had kept his hair closely cut, so that it was obvious how recently he had been one of them.

Seeing him to the door, the steward asked the customary question: "How did you come by your freedom?"

"A gift in my late master's will."

"Ah." He sounded wistful and looked approving. "May the omen be good."

Nikias walked home with a spring in his step, almost singing with satisfaction. He had done it, found a way into the Photionis stronghold. The Euthalion was only two nights away. In two nights, he would get inside that house, learn its secrets, and find a way to be something to the beautiful Kallion beyond just someone who sold him snacks every so often.

He shied away from thinking too hard about exactly what that might involve. If he let them, images would come crowding into his head: stroking the gentle waves of Kallion's hair, tasting his soft mouth, pushing up his tunic over a firm, slender thigh … Nikias felt stabbed with guilt, then remembered why he had no reason to feel disloyal now. And that just brought back the old, complicated ache.

It wasn't going to matter, he told himself, half to comfort himself, half in self-pity. He'd seen no evidence that Kallion found him even remotely interesting. Maybe they could become friends, and it would be one of those long, one-sided pining things. That would probably be for the best.

# CHAPTER 3

Pyke let Nikias have the afternoon off on the day of the Euthalion. "Go home and rest," she advised. "You're going to be up all night."

Nikias thought she seemed almost to approve of what he was doing—or what she thought he was doing. He wondered what she would have said if he had explained what he was really about. He had a feeling—he was getting a better sense of what Widow Pyke was like, under her prickly exterior—that she might actually have given him her blessing if she had known the truth.

Still, he didn't tell her, just in case.

"Are you sure you'll be all right on your own all afternoon?" he asked.

"I'll be fine. I'm not so feeble as all that yet."

"No, no, I didn't mean … er, well, thank you."

He went home and tried to take a nap, but he was too excited about the night to come. He went down to the bath house instead, spent a long time bathing, and then splurged at the barbershop, even though he wasn't really due for a haircut. Returning home, he put on his good tunic, fastened the belt that had been given him as a gift by his master's widow, and put in his favourite earrings (of the two pairs he owned). One of his neighbours, seeing him on the stairs, commented that he looked very spruce.

"You must have an invitation for the Euthalion," she said knowingly.

"No," he said, "a job."

"Ah! Even better." It was true. Paying work in the city was hard to find.

One of the things Nikias liked about his life these days was the walk from his home, in the cheap residential neighbourhood of West Vallina, down to the busy harbourfront street where Pyke's Snacks nestled in the corner of the Photionis mansion. He was usually walking in the other direction at this hour, with the sunset at his back. It was a spectacular one tonight, with long streaks of cloud catching the rosy light, and he felt his heart warm at the sight as if it were an omen of the night to come.

The city had that distinctive combination of hush and bustle that characterized a night of festivities. Many businesses had been closed all day in honour of the holiday, which had begun with parades in the agora in the morning, and now everyone was getting ready for their private parties. Lights were lit in all the windows, slaves were running in and out preparing, and in some streets you could hear musicians practicing.

Nikias thought about past Euthalions in his master's house. They had been small, cozy parties, but they had been highlights of the year all the same, times when the slaves were made to work hard but then given leave to enjoy themselves heartily too. Tonight, for once, he allowed himself the luxury of remembering all that with uncomplicated nostalgia.

He had been told to present himself at the kitchen gate, so he slithered down the alley again, careful to prevent his clean tunic touching the walls, and was met by a thin, unhappy-looking boy when he knocked.

"You one of the hired men?" The boy rolled his eyes as if to say *good luck*, and held the gate open for him.

"I'm to report to the steward. Do you know where I'll find him?"

"In the garden, I think. Come on, I'll show you."

The scene in the kitchen reminded Nikias of a painting his master had had on his library wall of Nepharos's hell for traitors: steam rising everywhere, fire crackling and spitting, half-naked slaves sweating and cursing and dodging around one another with pots and platters and dripping spoons. But it smelled much better than he imagined the scene in the painting would, and the food that was being whisked by and piled up and assembled looked elaborate and delicious. Nikias spotted several dishes that he would have loved to know how to make and felt a fleeting disappointment that he wasn't going to be working in the kitchen after all. He spotted Itia in the chaos and gave her a friendly wave as he followed the boy through the door into the colonnade surrounding the garden.

It was a good night for the Euthalion, the sky clear and the air warm but not hot. The garden, which was the biggest of its kind Nikias had ever seen, was decorated already with garlands of autumn flowers. Torches were lit, and striped pillows were scattered on the ground for guests to sit on. There was statuary in among the ornamental trees and flowerbeds, and a giant, ugly fountain in the middle of the garden. The boy who had let him in abandoned him to go back to his own work, which was irresponsible of him—letting a stranger wander around the house—but Nikias didn't object. He walked around the peristyle, looking for the steward. He didn't find him, but he found an iron gate beyond which, peering out of the darkness at him, he saw a huge cat, bigger than a dog, with a striped face and tufted ears. He jumped back in shock, then looked around shame-facedly, hoping no one had noticed.

When he had determined that the steward wasn't anywhere in the garden, he went into the house, through the open folding doors under the colonnade. A short passage opened onto a massive marble atrium. Nikias had had no idea the Photionis family was so rich. You couldn't tell from the street entrance, but their house was opulent beyond belief. There was gold everywhere, mosaics of semi-precious stones underfoot, huge mythological frescoes and shimmering curtains on the walls. Through the dining-room doors he glimpsed silk cushions, carved furniture, and more gold.

Nikias had grown up in a country villa, in the household of a minor Phemian nobleman. His master had always claimed that his lifestyle was very simple, but Nikias, having no basis for comparison, had never really believed that. Since coming to the city six months ago, he'd seen nothing to change his mind. Finally he understood, in a way that he never had before. This was the kind of thing his master had in mind when he said that he lived simply. These people were not even aristocrats—they were gangsters. But they were rich, and this was what their money had bought them.

This, and all the people coming and going through the glittering house, possessions of its master just as much as the wall-hangings and the couches and the big cat.

Nikias realized something else. Because he'd always naïvely imagined that he had grown up in a very grand household, it have never occurred to him to be nervous about serving in a mere townhouse. Now he realized that it should have.

Fortunately, it was too late to begin to be nervous now. The atrium of the house was full of people: two different groups of musicians, a knot of beautiful people who were probably dancers, several others carrying implements that Nikias imagined they might juggle later, and in the middle of all of them, a tall woman in a bright green dress, with elaborate loops and puffs of cherry-red hair, who was rattling off instructions to the steward. She must be the sister, the one Itia said had planned the Euthalion party. And the wan-looking blonde girl standing behind her was probably the widowed mistress of the house.

Nikias waited his turn and was assigned some duties eventually, which went like this: "Put him with Tiko, they'll look like a matched set. They can serve drinks in the garden."

Tiko, one of the household slaves, was a man in his thirties—a decade or so older than Nikias—with a weather-beaten look like an oarsman. Nikias didn't think they looked alike at all, except that they were roughly the same height and vaguely similar colours of brown. He wondered if Elpis even realized he had been hired for the night and wasn't part of her late brother's household.

He followed Tiko down into the cellar and was shown where to get the wine and given some rudimentary advice about serving, none of it news to him, though he listened patiently to it. They filled their wine jugs in preparation for the arrival of the guests.

"You worked one of these affairs before?" Tiko asked, leaning against the wall while Nikias filled his jug. "Me, I'm new to this house—came with Master Epaphras—so I've never done one of these."

"Me neither," said Nikias. "I'm just here for a little extra money."

"Yeah?" Tiko made a sympathetic face. "Guess you got to worry about that kind of thing when you're free. You ever sleep with a free woman, Nikias?"

"No, I … no." He was going to say that sleeping with women wasn't one of his interests, but he realized in time that might end with Tiko asking whether he'd slept with a free *man*, then, and Nikias didn't want to talk about that with a stranger.

"Me neither," said Tiko thoughtfully. "I'd like to, some day."

"Maybe when you're freed yourself," Nikias suggested.

Tiko chuckled. "Don't know that I want to wait that long. From all I hear, this would be the night to do it."

"Oh. Er, is that so?"

"From what I hear. I dunno, though. Whether I've got the nerve." He grinned. "She'd have to come on pretty strong, you know?"

"Right," said Nikias, trying, out of politeness, to sound like someone who discussed this kind of thing all the time. "Heh. Yeah."

Kallion had been looking forward to his first Euthalion not spent in Old Photis's house, but apparently that was not going to be this year's Euthalion. Epaphras had been very polite about asking him to come, kindly giving Kallion the option to refuse, but it was a good opportunity to make contact with the people on his list of Hesteus's debtors, possibly even to add a few names to it, and he couldn't in good conscience pass it up.

It was odd to arrive with the guests and not even see any of the preparations for the party, the frenzy of cooking and carrying and decorating and the yelling of abuse from almost every quarter. It felt wrong, even, as if he had become part of the problem for everyone else. He entered the house feeling apologetic and trying to take up as little space as possible.

He could not locate Epaphras on his first circuit around the party. It was very much an Elpis party, the kind she used to throw when her brother was alive. There were flowers and musicians everywhere, and guests were drinking hard already, laughing and lounging in the torchlit garden.

He saw plenty of familiar faces, of course, including a

couple who interested him. As luck would have it, one of them, Soukides, was high on his list of people to find. Kallion waited, sipping his wine demurely, while Soukides finished a conversation with another man, then stepped up beside him.

"May I speak with you a moment, sir?"

Soukides gave him the worried look that Kallion was used to, after four years of bearing messages from Hesteus Photionis.

"What is it regarding?" Soukides asked, clinging to his dignity.

"Something to—something that you will be glad to hear." He stopped himself in time from using the phrase *to your advantage*, which was usually a euphemism for something terrible. "I am acting on behalf of Epaphras Photionis, who is overseeing the disposition of his late brother's estate."

It didn't work. Soukides paled visibly. "Please—let us—let us speak privately."

"Certainly, sir." Kallion gestured toward one of the summer sitting rooms off the garden, half-drawing the curtain after them so that they could both see out and signal their wish not to be disturbed.

The moment he turned back to Soukides, the man launched into a plea for more time.

"It has become more difficult to raise the money each month, with business being as it is, and my wife's health—she's no longer able to work in the shop as she used to, and we've had to hire a girl—and of course the six months' reprieve has been a help, and we are very grateful—"

Kallion held up his hands. "Sir, sir, I'm not here to *ask* you for money. I want to *offer* you money."

Soukides's eyes darted wildly. "In exchange for what?"

"No, no. In compensation. Epaphras Photionis wishes to make some amends for the wrong done by his late brother. We can't return all the money you paid Hesteus, only a token sum, I'm afraid—but it comes with our assurance, with Master Epaphras's assurance, that you will not be asked for any more payments."

Soukides digested that for a moment. "He's really dead, then. He-Hesteus."

"We believe he is dead," Kallion temporized.

"And his brother, Epaphras, is he taking over the business?"

"Well, to some extent. He is … scaling back operations." *Hasn't the stomach for it*, was how some people, such as Elpis, put it. *Is a better man than his brother*, is what Kallion would have said. "He will no longer be providing the 'service' for which you paid Hesteus. But since that service was 'not having your shop burned down by men employed by Hesteus Photionis,' I think you will find you can do without it."

"He always said that there were other threats … " Soukides's voice trailed off. It was clear that he had never really believed it. "How much were you, er, thinking of offering?"

Kallion quoted a sum, and Soukides nodded.

At that moment the half-drawn curtain was jerked open, and a startled slave with a wine jug looked in.

"Oh! Excuse me." He took a step back, trying to replace the curtain, but it stuck on the rail, and he had to tug it for a moment.

In fact, he was not a slave; he was the assistant from Pyke's Snacks, the one who made such good octopus fritters. His behaviour—speaking to guests unbidden, barging in where he wasn't wanted—would never have been tolerated in a slave of this household, but he must have been hired for the night.

Nikias. His name was Nikias. He was Pyrian, with light brown skin and thick, dark hair that would have been furiously curly if he hadn't kept it cropped in an old-fashioned slave cut. He wore earrings, like most Pyrian men. And he really was cute: tall and burly, a little chubby, with big hands, an open, honest smile, everything about him wholesome and uncomplicated.

Kallion had noticed all this a long time ago. He couldn't remember now which he had noticed first: that the octopus fritters at Pyke's had improved, or that the young man who made them was a stunner. In any case, those had been two good reasons to stop at the snack stand more frequently in the last few months.

Nikias got the curtain to close after a moment and retreated with an embarrassed smile. Kallion turned just in time to see Soukides melting away.

"We will speak more," Kallion called after him encouragingly.

He wasn't sure whether that had been a success or not. It was not the first of these conversations he'd had, though, and he was beginning to get used to how they went. People who had spent any time under Hesteus Photionis's thumb were jumpy, nervous, reluctant to accept that things might be changing for the better. Kallion had lost count of the number of times he had been asked, "So is he really dead?"

He wished he had a better answer. He made an offering at the White Temple every first Moon's Day, praying for a better answer.

*Yes, he is dead. They found a body. Someone saw him die. The murderer has confessed.*

Well. He didn't really want that last one.

He went looking for Epaphras again, and again failed to find him in any of the public parts of the house. He spotted one of Epaphras's household slaves and asked him if he knew where his master was.

"At his own house," the man replied. "Satteia's back."

"Who?"

"Mistress Satteia. Master's wife."

"Blessed Orante! Is she really?"

The man nodded with obvious satisfaction at being able to relate this gossip. They were in a private corner, screened from the rest of the garden by a column and some climbing plants. The slave, whose name Kallion remembered was Tiko, had been taking a break back here, leaning on the base of the column. The party was becoming noisy, and many guests were seeking out such corners.

"She showed up on our doorstep here Market Day night," Tiko went on. "Word is, she's willing to give the marriage another try now that the brother is out of the picture."

"Yes, it was something to do with him, why they quarrelled, wasn't it?"

"Oh, as to that, I could tell you some stories! If you ask me, she was right to leave. People will say it was because Hesteus 'insulted' her, and he did that all right—he never liked her, never liked any woman with a brain—but that was the least of it. He used to treat their house like it was his own. Brought people there for meetings or to rough them up—kept a hostage in the cellar for a week, one time—got his brother in knee-deep in all kinds of shit, right? And the mistress knew what he was about, and she wasn't having it. She tried for years to get the master to stand up to Hesteus—stood up to him herself, by Anaxe's tits—but he'd never do it, or never do it any way that was worth shit, so she left."

"And now she's back." Kallion leaned on the column next to Tiko. "And Epaphras is at home with her instead of here."

"Wouldn't you be?" Tiko nudged him with an elbow.

For a moment, by chance, they were looking into each other's eyes.

"She's … not my type," said Kallion.

"Yeah? You got a type? Me, I'm not particular."

# CHAPTER 4

It was well past midnight, and Nikias understood why Itia had warned him away from this party. It had started out almost sedately, with important guests arriving first to fill up the dining room, and a steady stream of lesser people pouring in after them to mill about the atrium and flow out into the garden. Food went from the kitchen to the dining room, and empty dishes came back, and wine and snacks circulated everywhere.

Dinner finished and the serious drinking began. Some of the dining-room guests left, and some people came in off the street who had obviously started drinking somewhere else. The crowd contracted slightly, but it was still by orders of magnitude the biggest private party Nikias had ever served at. One group of musicians played in the house, another in the garden, and dancers and acrobats moved fluidly among the guests in a way that made the whole party feel like a staged spectacle, or maybe a dream.

Then some of the dancers began to shed their clothes, and Nikias realized with shock that they had been hired—or bought, or rented, or whatever it was—to do more than dance.

He stood in the colonnade with his jug of wine, looking out on the garden. Guests were shedding their clothes now too, and there were several naked bodies splashing in the central fountain. Nikias had cleaned up after three different people who had been sick in the colonnade, and he didn't think any of them had gone home. Guests had taken dancers and slaves into the bedrooms, in pairs and groups, and not troubled to close the doors. There was a cockfight going on in the atrium. On the other side of the garden, the gate to the wild-animal menagerie stood open, which meant that theoretically, a lynx could have been wandering anywhere in the garden or the house, though he hadn't seen it and supposed that might be because it had more sense.

He had seen a tiger, though it was chained up, and a giant snake draped on a tree limb, and he'd had to help Tiko and the steward pull a guest out of a pond that apparently contained a crocodile. He had asked why the gate to the menagerie was not kept locked for the night, and had been told that the mistress of the house had unlocked it on a bet.

Nikias had poured wine for the mistress of the house, and he didn't think that was true. He thought she had been bullied into it, and probably gave in only because she was very drunk. He'd heard her talking to the woman seated beside her, telling stories with a high-pitched, forced-sounding cheerfulness, about her late husband (though she never used that term). Nikias imagined his own master's widow talking like that—"My dear, you wouldn't believe some of the things he used to get up to"—and his stomach lurched with a mixture of disgust and disloyalty.

*All right, Nikias,* he told himself, *pull yourself together. It's a debauch, and you don't like it—no surprise there. You didn't come here to enjoy yourself, you came to find out what it was like, and now you have.*

It didn't help. His skin crawled and he felt dirty all over. Everything that he had always been told to despise about the decadent city was on display here, and he wished it seemed liberating, like a revelation about how the world really was outside of the bubble where he had been brought up—but it didn't. There was a feverish, cruel quality to it all.

He had seen Kallion several times since that awkward encounter behind the curtain. He always seemed to be on the edge of the party, wine cup in hand but talking seriously with someone, off in a corner. He didn't look like he was enjoying himself.

That gave Nikias hope, more than he liked to admit. Kallion was a decent man; of course he wouldn't enjoy himself at a party like this. But he was here, for some reason, and maybe there was something Nikias could do to help.

He had been talking about money with that man behind the curtain. Was he in need of money? That, admittedly, was not something Nikias could help with. But if it was something else …

Nikias pulled himself together and did another circuit of the garden with his wine jug. At the back of the garden, beside the long, narrow passage that led to the kitchen, were three open-air rooms, Nikias didn't know quite what to call them, done up to look like a city-dweller's idea of caves, with uneven stonework and creeping plants in badly disguised pots. The two smaller ones had curtains hung at the entrance, and it was in one of these that Nikias had encountered Kallion earlier. The curtains were drawn now, and he assumed that meant there were things going on behind them that he didn't want to see. There were people playing dice in the middle cave, and he had already topped up their cups. He looked around the garden to see if there was anyone else to serve.

He didn't see anyone who looked like they needed, or even wanted, more wine, so he started down the kitchen passage, headed for an alcove where garden tools were stored, which he had spotted earlier and mentally noted as a good place to duck out of sight and take a rest. He rounded the corner to find that someone was there before him.

It was Tiko, and he was not alone. He was perched on the edge of a wheelbarrow, head thrown back, eyes closed, knees spread, and kneeling between his thighs was …

Kallion. There was no way to doubt or deny it. Nikias backed away, almost slamming himself against the wall in his haste to get out of sight, but he'd had a full view of Kallion's face in profile, and he knew it was him. On his knees, in a dirty corner of the slave quarters, his beautiful white fingers curved around the base of Tiko's cock, his tongue coming out to lick the tip, tidily and carefully, the same way he ate octopus fritters.

And the worst of it was how good he looked there. Nikias knew he should have been shuddering in horror, but he wasn't. His own body was reacting, shamefully, with lust.

He could hear the words from that night four years ago, and the pain behind them: "No free man should willingly submit to that. It is a degradation of the worst kind." He could tell himself that wasn't true, he didn't believe that any more—hadn't really believed it then—but it didn't matter. He should not have been able to look at that—a free man on his knees in front of a slave—and find it beautiful.

He was aware that behind him, the noise of the party had changed subtly. Some new voices had been added. He forced himself to turn toward the garden and put one foot in front of the other, feeling numb and unreal. Someone scurried past him with a worried expression and a tray.

The newcomers, Nikias saw when he came back out into the garden, had come in the back door, from the private jetty in the harbour. They wore red sailors' caps and checked tunics, flashy and foreign. Their leader had a long black beard braided into two uneven tails and a short sword in his belt. They were laughing and calling loudly for wine.

The mistress of the house stood between two of her

friends, white-faced and dismayed but also swaying slightly, her dress falling off one shoulder, her hair coming down. Some of the guests were acting as if they knew the newcomers and hailing them heartily. Others, those who were still sober enough, began edging toward the house, murmuring excuses and talking about how late it was.

Nikias poured wine for a couple of the sailors, keeping his head down and his posture deferential. He wondered where the huge doorman was. They could have used him in here. They could have used Tiko, for that matter, if he hadn't been … Nikias reminded himself not to think about that.

The black-bearded captain was strolling around the benches by the fountain, looking over the female guests with a leer. Most of the women left in the garden by this time were slaves or hired girls or just very, very drunk. The captain stopped in front of a young woman in a short tunic. Nikias had seen her dancing earlier, but now she was sitting on the end of one of the benches, hollow-eyed with exhaustion, her bare legs stretched out in front of her, cradling a half-full wine cup. The captain plucked her cup from her hands and drained it in one gulp, then, as she made an aborted movement of protest, he shoved her back onto the bench. She started up with a cry, and was trying to push him away with her arms and legs as he bore down on her, laughing.

Nikias flung away his wine jug and didn't hear it fall. He tore around the edge of the fountain, guests scattering before him, and grabbed the captain from behind by his long, matted hair.

The man gave a startled bellow, arms flailing, unbalanced, and Nikias flung him sideways. The dancer rolled out of the way and scrambled up. The captain landed with a thud on his hip. There were shrieks and laughter from the guests.

For a moment the captain looked up at Nikias, wild-eyed.

"Goat-fucker!" he roared, and surged awkwardly to his feet.

Nikias punched him.

It wasn't a particularly good punch—he didn't know the first thing about punching people, really—but that probably just made it more humiliating for the captain, because it sent him flying. He hit the edge of the fountain, tipped over, and fell backward into the water with an impressive splash.

Everyone laughed, even the sailors who grabbed Nikias by the shoulders and the ones who dragged their captain dripping out of the fountain.

"You! Slave!" It was the party's host, the woman with the cherry-red hair, pointing at Nikias. "How dare you? You laid hands on one of my guests. I will have you flogged."

The captain shook water out of his eyes like a dog and grasped the hilt of his sword. "My men'll do it," he growled. "For a start."

"Anaxe's tits," Tiko groaned. "You're good at that."

"Well, you know." Kallion rocked back on his heels. "Practice."

"Yeah? Yeah, must be, huh?"

Tiko tucked himself back into his loincloth and stood. He was looking down at Kallion with a familiar expression— a pretty mild version of it, actually. Not disgust, exactly, just a slight discomfort at the idea that he'd had his cock sucked by a man who enjoyed it.

The moment was broken by someone running through the passage toward the kitchen calling, "The Dodeki are here!"

"Fuck," said Kallion. He got to his feet.

"The *Dodeki*?" Tiko repeated. "At a Euthalion party? I know they worked for Hesteus, but … "

"They have a standing invitation to the house." Kallion scrubbed his face with the heels of his hands. "I'd better go."

"You and me both."

Tiko rolled his shoulders and reached down for the wine jug that he had propped against the wheelbarrow. It had tipped over and spilled its contents on the pavement, though neither of them had noticed at the time.

"Thanks for—you know," Tiko said.

For a moment Kallion thought the other man looked like he might pat him on the backside. He would have liked that, actually. But it didn't happen.

They headed in opposite directions, Tiko back to the kitchen, Kallion, reluctantly, out to the garden.

The party was in upheaval. Some guests had obviously left, but the rest were crowded in the garden, where some kind of spectacle was apparently taking place. Something to do with the Dodeki. Kallion didn't like the sound of that.

He worked his way through the crowd until he could see what was going on. The Dodeki were here indeed, a whole crew of them, led by a youngish captain who called himself Skopo. All the new Dodeki captains had stupid assumed names to go with their stupid clothes and their swaggering, fire-breathing manner. They were dangerous, bloodthirsty men, and in his heart Kallion was as terrified of them as everyone else, but he had always found something ridiculous about them too.

Skopo stood watching while one of his men flourished a long whip, the kind used on galley slaves. Two other sailors were holding down a young man between them on the tiles by the fountain. His tunic was pulled up, and there were already several bright lines of blood across his light brown back. The whip whistled down and added another. The young man's body jerked, but he made no sound.

"What's happening?" someone near Kallion asked.

"One of the slaves punched the captain," someone else

replied. "Knocked him into the fountain! You should have seen it."

The whip cracked and whistled again. Kallion saw Rhoias standing with a couple of her friends, all of them looking sick and white. Elpis was calmly sipping her wine and looking satisfied with herself. Kallion looked down at the young man being flogged and saw the side of his face in the torchlight, the cropped dark hair, the gold earring.

"Stop this!" he shouted, striding forward out of the crowd before he could think too much about what he was doing. "Stop!"

The man with the whip glanced in his direction and laid down another lash.

"What did you say?" Skopo growled. "Are you telling my man what to do?"

Kallion gathered all the dignity he possessed, everything he had honed on the orator's platform as a youth, everything he had learned from watching Hesteus and his father before him, and faced the Dodeki captain.

"Yes, I am. I said, 'Stop.' This man is not a slave." He turned to the sailor with the whip. "Excuse me," he said calmly. "Put that down. You cannot flog a free man for assaulting your master. That is not how it works. Your master could bring charges, if he wanted, though since he's … a pirate … he may prefer simply to let the matter go."

The sailor lowered the whip, looking confused.

"You are on land now," Kallion said, slowly and clearly. "In your patron's house. You must obey the law."

He had nothing to back it up, just brazen attitude. They had weapons, swords and knives, every man of them. They backed down.

"Good," said Kallion crisply, as the sailors let go of Nikias.

The steward and Chares ran forward and helped Nikias to his feet and hustled him away in the direction of the kitchen. Skopo was glaring at Kallion and making a sort of sub-human growling noise, but when Kallion turned airily away from him—a feat which took a tremendous effort—the Dodeki captain contented himself with clouting one of his underlings and shouting for wine.

Kallion caught Rhoias looking at him, for a moment, as if she had seen a god walking the earth. Then she beckoned imperiously.

He knew what she wanted: for him to work his magic to get the Dodeki out of the house altogether. But he didn't have any magic left at this point; his knees felt weak. And he didn't owe her this. He held up a hand, a gesture with only a hint of apology, and walked out of the garden.

He went down into the cellar to pour himself a cup of wine, from the good stuff that wasn't being served at the party, and stood in a cool corner drinking it. He had not had much to drink at all that evening, but now he was ready to call it a night. All in all, it hadn't been a bad one. He had spoken to several of Hesteus's victims, promising reparations and offering reprieves, had an enjoyable encounter among the gardening tools that hadn't ended too badly at all (compared to some), and possibly—probably—saved that young man from Pyke's snacks from being messily murdered in the garden.

He wondered why Nikias had punched a Dodeki captain in the first place. Not that they didn't all deserve punching, but it wasn't exactly a wise move. He wished he'd seen it happen.

He took the tunnel under the garden and went up the back stairs to the kitchen to return his wine cup. It was relatively quiet in here now, the cooking over for the night, only a few slaves busy washing dishes, others sitting on the floor and leaning against the counters in poses of exhaustion.

Nikias was in a corner near the door, sitting on an overturned crate with his tunic in his lap, while Itia cleaned up his back, wincing as she worked. Chares, standing nearby holding a lamp for her, looked up and saw Kallion.

"Immortal gods, Kallion! They haven't killed you?"

"Not that I've noticed." Kallion grinned.

Itia *tsk*ed. "That was reckless. Both of you."

"Naw, it was beautiful," said Chares. "You should've seen it. Bastard went over into that fountain like—*SPLOOSH*—and then Kallion told him, 'You must obey the law.'" He chortled.

Nikias had not spoken, but he glanced between Kallion and the two household slaves, and Kallion could see realization dawning in his open, expressive face.

"You—you used to belong to this household, didn't you?" Nikias said.

Kallion nodded. "I was born here."

"He was always very grand," said Itia disapprovingly, "even when he was one of us. Sit still, Nikias, I'm not finished." She set aside her cloth and bowl and picked up a bottle of salve.

Nikias straightened his shoulders and winced. "Yes, ma'am." He looked up at Kallion. "Thank you for intervening back there. I'm very grateful. I—I think they … "

"No, no," said Kallion randomly, waving a hand. He didn't want to hear Nikias say, *I think they were going to kill me*. He didn't want to think about that right now. "It needed doing. You're—going to be all right?"

"I expect so. Itia's doing a good job looking after me." He smiled over his shoulder at her.

Kallion stood there, arms folded, not knowing what more to say but not wanting to leave.

"What made you hit Skopo?" he asked finally.

The boy's face contracted angrily. "He'd attacked a woman. One of the dancers. She's gone home now—well, back to her, you know, 'house,' or whatever they call it."

They called it a *brothel*, unless they were being excruciatingly coy. Kallion didn't say that.

"I hope she thanked you," said Itia, sticking the stopper back in her bottle of salve.

Nikias nodded. "She did. She said if I went round there, her mistress would give me money—which I don't need, but it's nice. To think that she would." He stood up, moving gingerly, and smiled down at Itia. "Thanks—it feels better already."

For a moment he stood there, nearly naked, his skin bronzed by the warm, flickering lamplight. Kallion had been thinking of him as a youth, but he wasn't; he was a man, tall and softly sturdy, his face looking older now that it was drawn with pain.

"You've got to let it heal now," Itia was saying. "Sleep on your stomach, and don't try to do anything stupid. Here, you'd better take the leftovers Chares wrapped up for you— you won't be able to work tomorrow."

"Yes, ma'am," said Nikias again. He tugged on his tunic gingerly, fastened his belt, and took the napkin-wrapped bundle that Itia handed to him. "Thanks for everything. And if you want to say 'I told you so,' you did, so you're entitled."

Itia ignored that. "It's a shame you won't be paid for all your work, but I suppose if you'd wanted to be paid, you shouldn't have attacked a pirate in the middle of the party."

"Look, I can probably—" Kallion started. He could talk to Epaphras, or even to Rhoias. They wouldn't begrudge the young man his money. "You ought to be paid. How much were you promised?"

"It's all right." Nikias looked at Kallion for a moment, a strange look, before his gaze dropped to the floor. "I—I didn't really take this job because I needed money, so it's all right."

It suddenly occurred to Kallion, out of nowhere, that there

was some obscure connection between Demokritos Theontiades attacking him in the street the other day and Nikias from Pyke's Snacks being here tonight. It had something to do with him.

"Can I walk you home?" he said.

He didn't know whether that had come out of his mouth without his volition, or he had intended to say exactly that when he came into the kitchen and found Nikias there. Now that he had said it, it seemed inevitable.

Nikias looked back up at him with surprise. "Yes, all right. Sure."

Immortal gods. It did have something to do with him.

# CHAPTER 5

THEY WENT OUT through the dark kitchen yard into the alley beside the house, and Itia latched the gate behind them.

"I think I'll be all right," said Nikias when they reached the street. He didn't sound very certain. "If you'd rather not … but I'd be happy for the company … "

"Where do you live?"

"West Vallina."

"Let's go."

They walked past the shuttered front of the snack stand and on up the street away from the harbour. Many houses still showed lit windows, and sounds of music and laughter filtered out to the street. It was not such a bad night to be out after dark.

"So," said Nikias, "how long have you been freed?"

"Since last Month of Birds. Half a year."

"Really? Me too."

"Just enough time to get used to it, not enough time to take it for granted. Eh?"

"Yes! Exactly."

"You're friends with Itia?" Kallion changed the subject.

"Yes, after tonight I'd have to call her a good friend! Before tonight, just acquaintances. She misses Pyria and likes to talk to a former countryman."

"You don't have her Pyrian accent. You must have been young when you left?"

"Five or six, when I was sold. I grew up here. Well, not here, in the city—at my master's villa in the mountains. I came to the city to look for work, after my master died. I wanted something that wasn't farm labour, and I like working with food." He shrugged, then gasped at the pain this caused. "Ugh, I'm going to have to stop doing that. Anyway, I wanted to see the city. I never had, growing up."

"And I've never seen the mountains." And he'd never really thought of wanting to. He was a creature of Pheme, through and through. "What do you think of the city?"

"I like it. There's a lot more to life in the city, isn't there? I mean, there are more things to choose from."

"Yes." After a moment, Kallion added, "It's also easy to choose badly. When you said, earlier, that Itia could say 'I told you so,' was it because she warned you not to get involved with the Photionis household?"

"Yes."

"Well. She was right. They have … a lot of dangerous associates."

"Mm. I realized that."

"I think you're all right, as things are. I wasn't trying to alarm you. The man you … er, punched into the fountain? He's a pretty minor figure in his world. So you were lucky, in a way. If that had been Kakos or Bakano or one of the other Dodeki captains, you might have to worry about reprisals, but with Skopo I think you should be all right. I think a fair few people have punched him and gotten away with it."

Nikias had stopped walking. Kallion turned to look at him. He stood in shadows cast by the light from an open door, looking down at the stones of the street. "I went there tonight because I wanted to find out what really goes on inside that house."

"Well, now you know. Pirates show up at their parties uninvited. It's ghastly. Hesteus was the real poison, and he's gone—dead—but the whole place is tainted. You should stay away."

"You—you don't have that option, do you?"

"I? Well, I was a child of the household, and Epaphras Photionis is my patron. I like him—I work for him now because I want to. I'm free. I can choose."

"Can you?" Nikias's dark eyes had come up and were fastened on him. "I'm sorry. I saw something tonight that I should not have seen, and I swore to myself that I would not speak to you about it, but … "

"Oh." Kallion could guess now. He could guess what Nikias had seen, and what he was driving at now. Nikias had obviously lived a sheltered life at this mountain villa and didn't know how to say what he wanted. "I can choose, Nikias. And so can you. Let's go back to your place, and … we can talk more about it."

Nikias looked up again, eyes wide with naïve surprise. "All right," he said eagerly.

Yes, all told it had certainly not been a bad night. And it looked like it might get better.

Nikias thought the dark streets between the harbour district and the Vallina Hill had never looked so beautiful. Somewhere in his mind, a voice from the past suggested that he was delirious with the pain in his back—which was intense —and the shock of what had happened at the party. He felt balanced on a knife-edge between lamplit joy and an abyss of sorrow.

He was walking through the dark, quietly festive city

with Kallion, and the world was glorious. Kallion was a freedman like him, which somehow made him all the more wondrous. They were getting further and further away from the cesspit of the Photionis house, and Nikias could almost imagine its influence fading, like a bad smell, as they walked.

Kallion had belonged to that household, with its cages of wild animals and its pirates and debauchery. Kallion had been on his knees among the garden tools. There must have been some reason, some dire need that forced him to do that. Kallion had said that when they got back to Nikias's room, he would explain, and then maybe there would be something that Nikias could do to help.

As they walked slowly through the streets, Nikias wanted to reach out and touch Kallion, just his pale wrist or his beautiful hand, but of course he restrained himself.

*How could you want to touch him after seeing what he did, how he debased himself?* Nikias told the voice in his head to shut up. It was a dead man's voice, after all.

Kallion had fallen into easy, inconsequential talk about the city, asking whether Nikias had been to this or that neighbourhood or monument yet. He had good advice about markets, particularly which specialty foods could be bought cheapest where. He was tailoring his conversation to Nikias's interests, Nikias realized. How urbane! Where had he learned manners like this?

Then Nikias remembered Pyke's story about Old Photis educating his slaves to enter them in contests, like horses or fighting cocks, and the abyss threatened to swallow him again.

"I looked at some apartments in West Vallina," Kallion was saying, "when I was in the market, and I liked it there—people are friendly, and you don't worry about crime like you would in some of the other low-rent neighbourhoods. Don't you find?"

"Oh. Yes."

"But there aren't many apartments big enough for a family. When you're wanting to move up in the world, you should think about the Tetrina. That's where I live now. Not," Kallion added quickly, "that I have a family. But it's a good place to find an affordable flat, and it's a nice place to live. The buildings are old, but they're well built, and because you're on the highest hill, if you get a balcony, the views are unsurpassed. And the breeze in the summer makes all the difference. Have you thought about looking for a job at one of the high-end restaurants?"

On second thought, some of Kallion's stream of talk might be nervousness. What did he have to be nervous about?

"Were you freed when your master died?" Nikias asked, then realized Kallion had asked him a question that he hadn't answered. "Oh. Er, no—that is, I did look for work at restaurants, but not the expensive places. My master kept a simple household, and anyway I didn't work in the kitchen all the time. I don't know how to cook anything fancy."

"Ah." Kallion was silent for a moment. Nikias stared at the side of his face, wanting to reach out and tuck a strand of his hair behind his ear. "You asked me a question. Yes— approximately. My late master left a letter of manumission among the documents in his study, and his brother Epaphras was gracious enough to execute it after Hesteus's death."

"Oh. My master just wrote it in his will. He, um." Nikias found he couldn't quite say it. "He knew when he was going to die."

"I see."

"Funny us both being freed around the same time! I never thought you were a freedman, either, I was so surprised. I guess they didn't make you cut your hair?"

"No, hardly anyone in the city does that to their slaves any more."

"That's good. It's … what's the word?" He tried to recall the term his friend Lysandros used. "Dehumanizing."

Kallion gave him a blank look. "If you say so. Why do you keep your hair short, then?"

Nikias ran a hand over his head, wincing as the movement sent a ripple of pain down his back. "I don't know what to do with my hair. It's curly, you know? It doesn't grow out the way yours does."

"Oh." Kallion opened his mouth and looked as if he was about to say, as people usually did when Nikias told them this, that surely there were some Pyrian or Gylphian barbers in Pheme who could help him out. But he didn't. "I see what you mean. About 'dehumanizing.'"

Nikias smiled at him with a warmth that might have looked alarming. He couldn't help it. "It's just my hair, though—otherwise, I've been lucky. I got to walk away, come to the city, and make a new life. This is my building." He stopped in front of the stairwell which opened onto the street at the side of the apartment block. "You'll come up?"

"Of course."

"I'm afraid it's on the fifth floor."

"Take it slow if you need to," Kallion suggested.

"Eh?"

"Because you're hurt."

"I keep forgetting that!"

He led the way up, past knots of people who had over-flowed onto the stairs from parties in the larger apartments. As they climbed, it got quieter. The rooms on the upper levels were too small to host parties, and from the sound of it, Nikias's immediate neighbours were all either out or already gone to bed. On the fifth floor, they turned down the narrow gallery and reached Nikias's door.

He unhooked his key from his belt to unlock the door, noticing that his heart was beating hard. He was nervous, both about what Kallion was going to tell him once they got inside, and, even more so, about the idea of having Kallion in his room. He hoped he hadn't left a mess when he went out.

He was relieved to see in the light from the open door that his bed, which was just a mattress on a low platform against the wall, was made, his clothes were hanging up, and his few belongings were tidy. He left the door open while he set down his bundle of leftover food and lit a lamp, moving slowly to avoid making too many faces of pain. Kallion stood just inside the door and unfastened his sandals.

The lamplight flickered over all the things in Nikias's room that pleased him when he came home to them: the brightly striped blanket on the bed, the shelf above it with a cracked painted cup in which he stored his earrings, the low table at the foot of the bed with a basket of fruit on it. The room was not much bigger than the interior of Pyke's Snacks, but Nikias was proud of it because it was his, the place he had chosen for himself.

"There's, um," he said as it occurred to him for the first time, "nowhere to sit, really."

"Quite all right," said Kallion.

Nikias stepped out of his own sandals and closed the door, which made the room seem even smaller. What were you supposed to do when you brought a guest into your home? Offer them food, that was it.

"Would you like an orange?" he asked, picking one up from the basket.

"No, thank you."

"I'm sorry I don't have anything to offer you to drink ... "

"Quite all right," Kallion said again.

He seemed to be waiting for something, and Nikias didn't know what to do next.

"So ... " they both said at the same time.

They laughed.

"You first," said Kallion.

"No—no, you first. Please."

"All right." There was a warm smile in Kallion's eyes that made Nikias feel as if his heart might explode. "So … what did you see?"

"I … what?"

"Tonight, before we left the house, you said you'd seen … 'something you weren't meant to see.' What was it?"

Nikias felt the blood draining from his face. Kallion was giving him a bizarrely encouraging look.

"I—I—" He had to answer. Kallion had put a direct question. He *had* to answer. "I saw you in that alcove, where they keep the tools. And Tiko. I saw—I saw what you were doing to him."

Kallion raised an eyebrow. "And you liked the look of it?"

"What?" Nikias yelped. "*Liked?* How dare you!" He'd never said anything like that to anyone in his life, but it popped out. Kallion looked as if he had been slapped. "Of course I didn't like it—I would never—it's completely—I just wanted to know the reason, so that I could help. I wanted—I hoped—you were going to tell me why you had to do that, to d-debase yourself, to … "

"Well," Kallion said icily. "I am glad we cleared this up. I wasn't *asking for your help*, you big waste of space. I was offering to suck your dick, because I thought it might be fun. Which, clearly, if you're going to be like that, it wouldn't be. So fuck you. Fuck your octopus balls, fuck this broom cupboard you live in, fuck you."

He grabbed his sandals by the straps and slammed the door behind him.

For a minute Nikias remained standing in the middle of the room. Then he took a step back and sat down heavily on his bed, groaning aloud at the pain in his back. His world was reorienting itself again, and he wasn't sure he had the strength for that right now.

He moved gingerly to stretch out on the bed and buried his face in his pillow.

# CHAPTER 6

Court Row was never very busy the day after the Euthalion. The advocates and jurists mostly stayed at home, if they could afford it. The clients who came out looking for someone to draw up a contract or arbitrate a dispute tended to whisper and wince at the sun streaming in the clerestory windows of the court buildings.

Kallion slouched at his desk in the clerks' hall, nursing his bad mood.

He could tell himself it had all been an unfortunate misunderstanding; he'd thought Nikias meant one thing, Nikias had thought he meant something else, all very awkward and silly. He could tell himself that he didn't want anything to do with a boy who would recoil from his desires like that. And he didn't—or he shouldn't have. He had to stop thinking about that soft belly, those thick thighs, how it would have felt to have one of Nikias's big hands firmly cupping the back of his head.

He had not been imagining it; Nikias had wanted him. Nikias was the sort of person whose thoughts showed in his face. He had wanted Kallion, until Kallion had disgusted him. And that, the more Kallion thought about it, made him disgusted with himself. He slumped lower in his chair.

The day dragged on, enlivened only by a couple of divorce contracts and a dispute over the upkeep of a shared privy. Kallion went home early and uncorked a bottle of excellent Xanos white to drink alone in his empty apartment.

The next day he was at the Shipyard Road house at his usual time, and stood for a few moments in the street watching the workers taking down the sign from above the shuttered front of Pyke's Snacks. He felt an absurd sense of loss, as if something was being taken away from him, and he couldn't explain why. Had he imagined that he would stop there and buy octopus fritters from Nikias just as before, as if nothing had happened?

Actually, yes, he had imagined that. He'd thought they would have a chance to go back to being friendly acquaintances—or at least acquaintances who had been on their way to being friendly. They had shared something, maybe not something good, but it hadn't seemed like an ending. To his surprise, Kallion realized he didn't want to leave it like this.

And now, of course, it seemed he wouldn't have a choice. He walked on into the familiar house, waving a half-hearted greeting to Dolon at the door.

"Master's in the garden room," Dolon told him. "*With the mistress.*"

Kallion looked at him. "You don't mean Rhoias, do you?"

"I do not." There was a gleam in the big man's eye. "I mean Satteia."

"So she's really back?"

"She is really back. Things are looking up, my friend. Things are looking up."

"What about the snack stand? It's closing?"

Dolon rolled his eyes. "Oh, you want to know about that, just follow the shouting."

There was indeed shouting, coming from Hesteus's

unused study at the far side of the atrium. When Kallion entered, he saw Pyke herself, squared off in a combative pose against Elpis.

"I don't know why you've let it come to this," Elpis was saying airily. "It was a simple request. The boy created a dreadful scene at our Euthalion party. You can't expect us to let him go on working outside our front door."

"No, I can't, can I? Can't expect anyone in this house to do a decent thing, can I? Well, I'm through. I'm an old woman, it's past time I closed up the shop for good. Now, do I have to take you to court to get back the rent I paid in advance?"

"No, no, of course not." Elpis waved a hand irritably. "Kallion, handle it, will you?"

"It's not my job any longer, ma'am," said Kallion, "but I can certainly do that."

Elpis looked at him, blinking, as if refocussing her eyes to see a free man where she was used to seeing a slave of her brother's household.

"It's such a silly thing," she said, shooting an aggrieved look at Pyke. "All I asked was that the boy apologize."

"You told me to fire him if he didn't," Pyke corrected her.

"I take it he didn't?" said Kallion.

"I told him I'd fire him if he did!" Pyke snapped.

"Utterly unreasonable." Elpis shook her head.

"What did he do?" Kallion asked.

"He ruined our party—assaulted a guest, an old friend of my brother's—"

"He punched a goat-fucker who was assaulting a girl!" Pyke cut her off.

"Yes, er, I know," said Kallion, "but—what did he do when you told him not to apologize?"

"He quit."

That made sense. Kallion thought it was probably what

he would have done under the circumstances. Though he couldn't easily imagine himself being in those circumstances.

"The poor boy could barely move after the beating he took at the hands of your brother's 'old friend'—"

"It wasn't a 'beating.' He was flogged for—"

"You don't just flog people! He sent round to apologize to *me* for not turning up to work, and of course I close up the shop to go to check on him—the poor boy doesn't have anybody in the city—and as I'm leaving, who should come out her door but Mistress Elpis herself, to tell me I should make Nikias apologize. Apologize! *Tcha!*"

"And now I'll have to find a new tenant, and she wants her rent back." Elpis rolled her eyes.

"You could just … let her stay," Kallion suggested.

"Of course not!" Elpis snapped. "How would that look?"

"Don't try to talk her out of it," said Pyke. "I'm ready to leave, as a matter of fact. Only kept the place going because of Nikias, really." She gave Elpis a poisonous glare. "Not that I'd expect him to stay after all that. No, I was going to close up six months ago, but then Hesteus croaked—"

Elpis made an offended noise.

"—and Nikias showed up looking for work, and I thought, maybe it'll be a new era. Maybe I can keep this going a while longer. Well, that's that. I'm going to help my sister look after her grandkids. That will keep me busy."

Pyke went out to supervise the dismantling of her shop, and Elpis gloomed off elsewhere in the house. Kallion wrote up a credit note for the rent Pyke had prepaid on the corner space—a huge amount considering the size of the property— and went through to the garden to find Epaphras.

He had forgotten all about Satteia by this time, so it was a shock to see her lounging next to her husband in the garden room, gorgeous in a rust-coloured mantle and big gold earrings.

She must have seen his surprise, because she laughed. "You hadn't heard that I'm back?"

"I took it for a rumour," he said urbanely.

He glanced at Epaphras and could see why Dolon had said things were looking up. Kallion couldn't remember when he had last seen the man looking so happy.

And he was doing his best to look appropriately unhappy when he said, "This business with Pyke's Snacks, Kallion, it's very unfortunate."

"I'm sorry, sir. It is my fault—I advised you to make over the rental income from the corner property to Elpis. It never occurred to me that she would turn out her tenant. But she's quite adamant—and, unfortunately, within her rights."

"Oh, I know. It's not your fault. Please don't think that."

"I hear you're doing well, Kallion," Satteia said. "Working as a clerk in the law courts?"

"Distinguishing himself," Epaphras put in cheerfully.

"I hope I do not disgrace my patron," said Kallion with a bow.

"Sit down, Kallion," said Epaphras. "Can I send someone to bring you a drink?"

"He's here on business," Satteia pointed out, indicating the scroll in Kallion's hands.

"Oh, yes, that reminds me," said Epaphras.

Kallion perched on the edge of a chair and looked attentive.

"Do I own a bunch of ships, Kallion?"

"Er, yes, sir."

"Not the Dodeki ships—other ships. I found a lot of paperwork in my brother's desk about purchasing ships, building ships, hiring crew—but not pirates, apparently, honest men. Do you know what that was about?"

"It was a project he was working on," said Kallion, deliberately vague. "It never came to fruition, but I believe the ships are mostly built, and mostly paid for."

"Right. Well, can we sell them, then? I don't need ships. I don't even want the pirate ships, let alone a lot of other ships."

"We will have to finish paying for them before we sell them."

"Yes, of course—do that. And then get rid of them, if you don't mind. I mean—" Epaphras held up a hand as if to stop himself. "If you could find out how I should go about paying for them and selling them, I would be very grateful. Of course none of this is your job any more."

"Now *I* want to talk to you about something," said Satteia, to Kallion's surprise. "I want you to advise me."

"Satteia wants to invest in a business," Epaphras said proudly, "and I said you could draw up the contracts and so on for her. Eh?"

Nikias had spent the better part of two days lying on his stomach on his bed, getting up only to hobble to the privy and to argue with Pyke about quitting his job. By the evening of Market Day, he was desperate to get out, and made his way stiffly down to the wine shop on Armoury Street.

That night, he was there strictly to drink. Sometimes he went to see his friends, sometimes to listen to the debates. He never actually debated, but he did like to listen.

The Armoury Street wine shop was a dirty hole in a wall in Lower Goulina, where a group of anti-slavery radicals held their meetings. Nikias had stumbled across them once by accident, his second week in the city, and his reaction to them had from the beginning been complicated.

He'd discussed it over and over since then, but he got into it once more that night, after a couple of cups of wine, sitting across a small table from his friend Lysandros. It was a nice distraction from his other feelings.

"Because *my* experience of slavery wasn't so bad. It was all I knew, my master was good to me, and like a—like a—"

"Father?" Lysandros suggested dryly, swirling the wine in his cup. This was far from the first time he had heard this from Nikias, and Nikias was sure he wasn't the first person to say things like this to Lysandros, either.

He shook his head decidedly. "No, not a father. Just—my master. I didn't think of myself as entitled to freedom. *Which* —" He slapped a hand on the table. "—*was wrong.*"

Lysandros leaned back, chuckling. "I don't know why you don't get up and speak to the assembly some time, Nikias. Your oratory is—"

"Shut up."

"No, I'm serious. It's heartfelt. You're not dealing in abstractions—or not dealing wholly in abstractions. You have your experience, and you have your conviction about what is right and wrong—"

"And I have to—" Nikias slotted his thick fingers dramatically together, almost knocking over his wine cup. "Put them together. What's the word?"

"Reconcile?"

"That. And it's not easy. Mind you, most of the time I don't sit around thinking about this—most of the time I think about frying cheese pastries and whether I've got time to lift a few weights at the gymnasium after work, but every so often? I find myself thinking about it. Something will remind me of him, and I'll remember—or it's like I hear it, like a voice in my head: 'That was wrong. It didn't *seem* wrong at the time, but it was.'"

"You didn't do anything wrong," Lysandros clarified.

"No, no. I know that."

"Nor need you feel diminished, even now, for the wrong done to you still to be considered wrong. If someone stole from you, and you didn't notice that something had been taken, it still would have been wrong for the thief to take it."

"Yeah, yeah. You philosophers really get off on stating the obvious."

Lysandros laughed explosively. He was an actual philosopher—taught at the famous school on the agora where Nikias's master had gone as a boy—but he also hung around the crowd at the Armoury Street wine shop, their unofficial leader, as if he were equally comfortable in this company. More comfortable, maybe. He had frankly befriended Nikias on the first day Nikias showed up, baffled and more than a little upset by the discussions going on around him. Lysandros was good-looking, with his mop of curly hair and his dark eyes, but he had a reputation for complete, even bizarre chastity, and Nikias had still been too raw from his own loss when they met to feel anything but friendship for him.

"It isn't obvious, though," said Lysandros, sobering. "Or as obvious as it should be. You will hear the experience of slaves who have been 'well-treated' paraded as justification for the institution of slavery. I have heard it often."

Nikias nodded glumly, his bright, combative mood draining away. "I know. The world's rotten, isn't it, Lysandros?"

"Uh … yes? But why so especially now?"

"I don't know. Everyone is just awful to everyone else, and even when you try to help, it all goes wrong. You punch a pirate, you lose your job. Quit your job, whatever. Somebody offers to—to suck you up—off? I think it's 'off.' And you say no, and they're insulted, and it's all awful."

"Hm," said Lysandros. "I have not … had that precise experience, myself. Did it happen to you? The, uh, second part—you already told me about the pirate."

"Yes!" Nikias buried his head in his hands. "I'm such an idiot."

"I'm going to need more information before I can offer

my judgement on that. Can I assume you dislike the individual in question?"

"No! No, I like him a lot. I thought—there could've been something … But I couldn't let him—I mean, I didn't want it just then, it wasn't what I was expecting, but even if it was, how could I let him degrade himself like that?"

"Whoah, whoah, whoah," said Lysandros, holding up his hands. "That word—"

"Don't"—Nikias slapped a hand on the table—"start splitting philosophical hairs with me, you … you wretch."

"We really need to work on your insults," Lysandros undertoned.

"You know what I mean. He's a freedman, and when you're *freed*—you say it yourself all the time—you have to act like you're *free*, which means—"

"Hold on, that is not what I say all the time. I say, 'You *are* free.'"

"Right, so you have to act like it! You don't have to submit to the things a slave has to submit to, and you shouldn't."

"Unless you want to."

"But—that's—my—point. You shouldn't want to."

"Hm," said Lysandros.

Nikias frowned at him. "Is that all you've got?"

"For the moment. More wine?"

"Please."

When Lysandros had refilled their cups, he said, "You agree that we are all equal—enslaved and free, there is no *real* difference in worth between any two humans?"

"Of course."

"Then why is it permissible for someone in a state of enslavement to desire something that is forbidden to someone who is free?"

" … what? Oh, come on! I didn't say it was fine to want

to do that even when you're a slave—obviously it must be bad then too, if it's bad when you're free."

"Is it?"

"Apparently." Nikias shrugged, then regretted it, as usual. "I just … " His voice trailed off, and he finished in a whisper, "I just couldn't do that to someone … again."

Lysandros kindly did not ask what he meant by that.

# CHAPTER 7

IT WAS late evening by the time Kallion stood outside the apartment building on the Vallina where he had gone in a very different mood two nights earlier. He hadn't exactly hurried, but he hadn't dragged his heels aggressively enough either, and the hour was not yet so late that he could turn away and come back tomorrow. Or, better yet, find someone who could give the damn contract to Pyke and let her deliver it herself. He wished he had never mentioned that he knew where Nikias lived.

When he had climbed the stairs and found the door—he remembered the door, it had a charm hanging on it with a bead in the shape of a cat head, which he had thought adorable two nights ago—luck seemed finally to be on his side. There was no answer to his knock.

He stood there a minute or two for form's sake, gave another perfunctory knock, and touched a fingertip to the cat charm's nose. Then he turned to leave.

Nikias was standing at the top of the stairs. He hadn't seen Kallion yet; he was leaning heavily against one hand on the wall, eyes closed, obviously tired and in pain.

"Nikias," said Kallion briskly. Better to get this over with.

Nikias's eyes popped open. They looked slightly unfocussed. Immortal gods, he had been drinking. (Of course he had been drinking; in his situation, who wouldn't?) *Please let him not be drunk.*

"What do you want?" He sounded merely tired.

"I've come with an offer. Not—from me. From Satteia, Epaphras Photionis's wife. She wants to help you set up in business. If you want."

Nikias peered at him doubtfully for a moment, glanced around the gallery as if confused, then looked back at Kallion.

"What?" he said finally.

"Look, uh." He wanted to suggest they sit down somewhere, but the only place was inside Nikias's room, on Nikias's bed. And no. "How's your back?"

Nikias raised one eyebrow in a way Kallion hadn't seen him do before. It was remarkably charming.

"Stiff. Itchy."

Kallion winced. "Yes, the itching is the worst part, almost, isn't it?"

"Is it."

"Er, as I was saying, Satteia heard about the trouble Pyke had, and how you have left her employment, and she wants to help you open a snack stand of your own. Not in the form of charity, of course. She wants to offer you a sum to help establish your business, in return for a share of the profit. This is—I was interested to learn—something she has done before. She owns a share in a bakery, a glassworks, and an import-export business."

"And she wants to own a snack stand."

"A share in a snack stand, yes. She thinks you could open in the Tetrina Market—that's near where I live. It's an excellent idea because there's no one selling snacks there, and it's a busy market. She has some ideas about what you could sell and so on." Kallion wished this conversation would end. It was becoming more and more absurd. And some of it was veering into untruths. These had not been Satteia's ideas. "Obviously you will have to meet with her in order to discuss the details, but she wanted me to bring you the contract and go over it with you … Perhaps you'd better come see me at the clerks' hall in Court Row tomorrow. We can talk then."

"Yeah," said Nikias leadenly. "That would be better."

That *would* be better, and it could have been conveyed in a message; there was no need for Kallion to have come here himself. He cursed himself for not thinking of that.

They remained standing there awkwardly. Kallion would have to pass Nikias to get to the stairs, and Nikias was not moving.

"I'm not going to invite you in," Nikias said finally.

"No! What? No, of course not."

Nikias moved out of the way of the stairs, and Kallion rushed overeagerly toward them.

"Good night!" he called without looking back.

Nikias woke the next morning with a headache. He didn't think he had drunk all that much the night before, so this just seemed insulting. He lay in bed looking at the sun coming in his small window and hitting the floor in a bright square, remembering his conversation with Kallion.

If he hadn't seemed enthusiastic about Satteia's proposal last night, it was only because it had been delivered by the last person he wanted to see or even think about. As far as the proposal itself, he was all for it. The Tetrina Market sounded like a perfect location; he hadn't visited it yet himself, but somebody had been telling him all about it … Oh. That had been Kallion.

Lysandros had done that thing that philosophers always seemed to want to do, and got Nikias to see things upside down and backwards. He realized he'd been a sanctimonious prick, pretending that he knew what Kallion should and shouldn't be ashamed of, and he owed Kallion an apology.

He hauled himself out of bed, finding that his back was less stiff than yesterday, dressed, and set off for Court Row.

He'd never been here before, and didn't know what to expect, but it turned out to be a long, arcaded building running down one side of a narrow street next to the imposing bulk of the Hall of Justice. Inside the arcade were lawyer's offices, their names and symbols—a sword, a crow, a balance, and so on—painted on signs beside the doors. Nikias asked a messenger boy whether he knew where to find Kallion, and was directed to an arch at the end of the arcade.

Beyond the arch was not an office but a large hall, airy and pleasant, with clerks' desks arranged in rows, occupied by young men busily writing and talking to clients. The murmur of conversation was like the sound of the sea, and the room smelt pleasantly of wax and paper. Tall book-cupboards filled with scrolls lined the walls.

Kallion's desk was halfway down on the side of the room near the door. His head was bent over some document, but there was no one else at his desk. Nikias approached.

Kallion didn't look up, just went on working. He was writing in ink, consulting a tablet beside him that was filled with something that looked more like scribbles than writing. His hair was tied back, out of his face, exposing the delicate curves of his ear.

"Oh, hello." He looked up, an automatic smile on his face. Nikias felt as if he might melt. "Nikias. Hello." The smile faded a fraction, and Kallion gestured at a stool on the other side of his desk. "Have a seat. I'll—um, be with you in a minute."

"Sure," Nikias mumbled. "You look busy."

He pulled out the stool and sat gingerly, hoping it didn't creak. It didn't.

"Do you buy the furniture?"

Kallion looked up with a perplexed frown as Nikias was wondering why on earth he had said that.

"Um. It's hired."

"Oh. Just—it's a good stool. Sturdy. I'm pretty big … "

There was a pause. Kallion's tongue flicked over his lips. "You are, yes."

He looked back down at his paper—just stared at it, not writing.

"Look, I'm sorry," Nikias said, his voice coming out too loud.

Kallion looked up, simple annoyance in his expression. He slapped the tablet shut and put down his pen.

"I'm sorry for being such an ass the other night," Nikias went on quickly.

Kallion's eyebrows rose. "Oh. That. You don't need to apologize. There was a misunderstanding. You articulated something that—"

"I whatted?"

"Said. You said something that lots of people—most people—think." He shrugged. "You don't need to apologize for that."

"No, I do. All the more so because most people think that way. Most people are *wrong* about things like that."

"Uh. Are they?"

"Yes."

Kallion spent a moment carefully rolling up the scroll on his desk.

"So," he said finally, "yesterday evening, when we were alone outside of your room, that would have been a good time to talk about this. Today, here, would be a good time to talk about Satteia's contract—but less good for this."

Nikias laughed. "Yeah, all right. I see what you mean."

"Good."

Kallion reached down into a cubby under his desk and

withdrew the scroll he had brought to Nikias's apartment the night before—or anyway Nikias supposed it was the same scroll, as he hadn't taken a very good look at it last night. Kallion unrolled it on the desk and stared at it for a moment.

"Right. So. I'll read it to you, shall I?" He flicked a questioning glance from under his long lashes. They were being so careful to avoid offending each other now, and there was just the barest chance that Nikias might know how to read.

"Thanks."

"So the first part is standard language for this kind of contract," Kallion began. "It says—"

"You!" someone yelled from behind Nikias.

He swivelled on his stool to look behind him, shocked. A young man in a dirty tunic stood there, trembling with rage as he pointed a finger at Kallion.

"Agron," said Kallion calmly, rising from his desk. "How can I help you?"

"You, help me?" Agron growled. He gave a despairing laugh. "That's a good joke. Do you know how you could help me?"

He advanced around the desk, giving Nikias a wide berth and bouncing a little on his feet like a boxer. Kallion stood his ground, his posture tense but his expression cool.

"You could help me by dying in a ditch! You could help me by—Let go of me!"

Nikias had reached across the desk to grab the young man by the shoulder. He pushed him firmly back, swung around the desk, and got an arm securely across the fellow's chest.

"He ruined me!" Agron yelled, his voice ragged with emotion. "Everything I had—*everything* ... "

He must have been a boxer, or a wrestler or something; he was very hard to hold onto, although Nikias was the bigger of the two. It didn't help that the struggle was putting strain that Nikias didn't need on his injured back.

"I know," said Kallion seriously. "And I am sincerely sorry."

"That—doesn't—help!" Agron panted.

Nikias heard someone calling for guards, as everyone else in the hall stared and pointed at the commotion.

"I know," Kallion said again. "And I know it won't help for me to tell you that I had no choice. But what can I do now? Is there anything I can do now?"

"Now you can DIE AND GO TO HELL!"

Agron kicked out at Kallion's desk, sending it over in a shower of tablets and scrolls, and wrenched free from Nikias's grip. He scrambled over the fallen desk as Nikias dodged around it, and made a grab for the nearest weapon, which was the stool that Nikias had been sitting on. Nikias ploughed into him just as he threw the stool, hitting him full speed with his right shoulder. He heard the stool crash as Agron went over like a chopped tree.

By this time, guards from Court Row were coming in through the door, and a couple of other clerks hauled Agron up, blinking as if half stunned. Kallion was on the floor, but he was sitting up.

"Are you all right?" Nikias asked.

"Just slipped and fell avoiding the stool." Kallion gathered himself up and got to his feet. "Nice work, thanks."

Nikias rolled his shoulder, which hurt. His back was stinging ominously, too.

Two guards had arrived, and they escorted Agron out, slumped limply between them.

"What set *him* off?" one of the clerks near Kallion asked.

"He was a client of my late master," said Kallion, his voice flat. "He was not treated fairly."

"You'll press charges, of course?" someone else asked.

"I'll consider it," said Kallion, and Nikias guessed that meant, "No."

The others drifted away to return to their own business

when it became clear that they were not going to get any more information than that. Kallion looked at Nikias.

"Are *you* all right?"

"Eh. Have a feeling I'm going to start bleeding through my tunic in a minute, which will look bad—but otherwise." He stopped himself just in time from shrugging. "We'd better get this mess cleaned up."

Kallion gave him a tired smile. His hair was coming out of its neat ponytail, and Nikias almost felt as if he could have reached out and tucked it behind Kallion's ear, without it being strange. He found he still wanted to do it.

They gathered up the scattered documents and righted the desk. Kallion produced a satchel and put several scrolls into it.

"I just bought this. I thought it might come in handy if I'm ever attacked in the street again."

Nikias snorted. "In case I'm not at hand to gather up your things for you."

"I'm going to call it a day, you may not be surprised to hear. There's a physician in the street behind Court Row who could take a look at your back. My treat?"

"Sure," said Nikias. "Let's go."

# CHAPTER 8

"I'll walk you home," Nikias said as they left the physician's shop. His back, which had indeed begun to bleed again, was freshly bandaged.

"All right," said Kallion easily. "Then we'll be even."

"No chance," said Nikias. "That pirate was going to kill me if you hadn't stopped him. You just got a stool thrown at you."

"A good, sturdy stool."

Nikias sputtered with laughter. "Yeah, but I didn't stop that happening. Where do you live? Oh, you said the Tetrina Hill. Um." He turned around in the street. He was in an unfamiliar neighbourhood and couldn't see any landmarks, so he had no idea which way to go.

"This way," said Kallion, nodding up the street.

They walked slowly, sticking to the less-travelled back streets. Kallion seemed to know lots of shortcuts, leading Nikias down crooked alleys that looked like they went nowhere but turned out to take them in exactly the right direction. For a while they didn't talk.

"I guess … " Nikias said finally, "that fellow blamed you for something that was really your master's doing?"

Kallion sighed. "It was my *doing*. I was the one who ruined him. Though … the one who bore him ill will was my master, yes."

"You know that's not the right way to look at it. You did what you had to do."

"No. It's only now, as I'm trying to repair some of the damage, that I can see all the other things I *might* have done, if I'd had the courage, or, I don't know—the hope? If I'd believed it could make any difference. But I didn't."

Nikias didn't think that was fair, and it made him sad to think of Kallion bearing that kind of guilt for things he was forced to do. But he didn't argue. He knew well enough the way that slavery warped your view of the world and your own place in it.

For the past six months, the place that Kallion had called home was an apartment at the top of a three-storey building on a quiet street on the summit of Tetrina Hill, right next to the park. Some of his windows even looked out onto trees, and he could hear birdsong in the mornings. He was very proud of his apartment. He'd never had anyone over to visit.

Standing at the bottom of the stairs, at the back of building, he couldn't decide what to say.

"Well, I'll just—" Nikias started, taking a step backward, after the silence had dragged on too long.

"You need to look at—I mean, we need to go over the contract."

"Oh, right. And make my mark, or something, right?"

"Well, that will be later, but—come up?"

"Sure," said Nikias, with just a slight hesitation.

Kallion led the way up the stairs and unlocked his door. He ushered Nikias in. Nikias looked around appreciatively. Kallion's apartment was like a little house of a classic plan, the front room proportioned like a small atrium, with a high ceiling and mosaic floor. The walls were painted with black and white panels in the middle of which floated small, delicately rendered still-life scenes. Kallion had not chosen the decorating scheme himself, but he loved it.

There was a study in one corner, behind an arch, with bookcases and a writing desk. A matching arch on the opposite side of the atrium led to a small dining room. The passage that would have led to a garden if this had been a house on the ground ended instead in a set of louvered shutters concealing the balcony.

Nikias had turned around to look at Kallion. "This is gorgeous. How … " He swallowed the rest of the question, which, Kallion assumed, was going to have been, "How do you afford this?"

"Let me show you around," Kallion said, although you could really see most of the apartment from the front door. And of course he wasn't going to go near the bedroom.

He showed off his study, opened the shutters that overlooked the park so that Nikias could marvel at the view, and led the way toward the balcony, pointing out the tiled bathroom to the right. But what really interested Nikias, Kallion realized when he saw where he had stopped and heard him gasp, was the doorway opposite the bath, which led to the kitchen.

"Is that—do you—"

Nikias stepped in and reached almost reverently for the faucet above the sink. He turned the handle, and gave a little squeal when water came out.

"Running water! On the third floor!"

"I know, isn't it nice? It's in the bath, too—that's one of the reasons I took this place."

Nikias was looking around the kitchen, mouth slightly open. "You don't cook, at all, do you?" he said, running a finger over the untouched surface of the stove.

"What makes you think that?" Kallion asked wryly.

"Uh … there's no food in here—not even a single pot. Oh, you have a few dishes," he remarked as he found them sitting lonely on a shelf, "and—immortal gods, that's a lot of wine." He stood looking into the pantry.

"It's an average amount," said Kallion defensively. "Maybe a little above average." He tried to think of some excuse for it—that he entertained a lot, or received a lot of gifts of wine, maybe, but neither of those things was true.

Nikias turned back to look at him. "Do you think … " He shook his head, as if to dismiss some thought. "Right. Well, we'd better look at the contract, hadn't we?"

They sat in Kallion's study—Nikias in the lone chair, Kallion on the edge of his desk—and Kallion read out the contents of Satteia's contract and explained some of the technical terms. Nikias listened carefully.

"Do you think I should sign?" he asked, when Kallion had finished.

"Do I … "

"I mean, do you think I should go into business with Satteia? I've only met her once. Do you think I'd be wise to trust her?"

Kallion considered. "I think you can trust her, yes. I even think she's a good businesswoman, and you could do very well partnering with her. But … she is a member of her husband's family. She could have tried to divorce him, but she never did, so they are still legally married. And, well, you know what I think about people getting involved with that family."

Nikias nodded, looking down at the contract. "I think that ship has sailed, honestly. Where do I have to sign?"

"Oh, you don't have to sign now. You'll meet with Satteia and both sign it. I will tell her you've accepted." Kallion got down from his desk. Suddenly he didn't know what to say.

A drink, that was it. He should offer Nikias a drink. And

show him the view from the balcony—they never had made it out there.

Nikias pushed back Kallion's desk chair and stood. "I'd better get going. Pyke offered to give me some of her old pots, and if I'm really going to do this, I'd better go round to her place and make sure she hasn't given them away to her sister."

"Oh—right."

"Thanks … for all this."

"I didn't do anything. Did I do anything?"

"Sure, you wrote the contract, right?"

"Yes, I did do that. But that's my job. Not that … I'm happy to have helped, if this is something that you want."

"It is."

"How … how's your back?"

"Calmed down again. How about you?"

"Me?"

"You got—you know, with the stool?"

"I'm fine."

"I guess you're used to that sort of thing. People blaming you for things that your ex-master did. Or does it only happen when I'm around?"

"No," Kallion admitted, "and it's not things my master did—at least not in this case."

"It's something he made you do."

Kallion shook his head. "Not exactly. Agron … was in a position to be inconvenient to my master—very inconvenient—and what usually happened to people in that position was that they'd be found dead. But he had a young family, and he wasn't really dishonest himself. I gave him some advice—I said it came from my master—but it was bad advice. He followed it, and he was ruined."

"So … he wasn't inconvenient to your master any more," Nikias guessed. "So he's still alive."

"Mm."

"So, actually, you saved his life. And his family and everything."

"Maybe. His family probably suffered when he lost all his money. It wasn't ideal."

There was a long silence. Nikias was giving him a strange, intent look.

"I was thinking—" Kallion started.

"After I get Pyke's pots," Nikias said at the same moment, "can I—oh, sorry. What were you going to say?"

"No, go ahead."

"Uh. Can I come back and make you dinner?"

Kallion stared at him. That was entirely unexpected.

"I—yes. I was going to ask if you'd like to come back some time to use the kitchen. To test recipes or anything. It doesn't have to be tonight."

"But can it be?"

"Sure. Yes. That would be—I'll be looking forward to it."

Nikias laughed a little awkwardly. "Me too! Thanks for— it's kind of you to think of it. It'll be a treat to use that kitchen. Right, I'll be back around twelfth hour, if that's all right."

"Yes, uh, absolutely."

Kallion stared at the door after it closed behind Nikias, and after a moment, slowly and with a feeling that might have been relief, he began to laugh.

# CHAPTER 9

NIKIAS PICKED up the pots from Pyke, and they had a long conversation about his new business prospects, with her giving him all kinds of advice. He spent the rest of the afternoon shopping and planning what he would cook for dinner.

It was all very well to tell Kallion that he just wanted to use his kitchen; of course he also wanted to impress Kallion. He had wanted that for a long time, and even though their circumstances had changed so much in the past few days, he found he still wanted it.

He left the market with salt fish, bread, eggs, oil, salad greens, olives, honey, some extravagantly expensive hard cheese, milk, and a very small packet of peppercorns which had cost almost as much as the cheese. Laden with all of this plus one of Pyke's pots, a pan, and a couple of trusty utensils from the snack stand, he made his way back to the top of the Tetrina Hill and Kallion's front door.

Kallion answered to his knock, looking like someone who had spent the afternoon relaxing. He was wrapped in a plain blue-and-white mantle, his long hair pulled back from his face with a soft band of blue cloth. The ends were wet, and a subtle scent about him suggested that he had just bathed.

"Here, let me take some of that," he said, reaching for some of Nikias's burdens.

He followed Nikias into the kitchen, and they set everything on the worktop.

"So you got the pots from Pyke?"

"I did, yes. Not the really good one I was hoping she would give me, but a bunch of others. I took most of them home—my room is full of cookware."

After a moment, looking around the kitchen, Kallion said, "Is there anything I can do to be helpful, or shall I leave you alone to enjoy the kitchen?"

"Oh, I have everything I need, I think. Are you hungry? I can start right away, and it won't take long."

Kallion chewed his lip as if he didn't want to admit that he was ravenous. Nikias wondered whether he'd eaten lunch.

"I'll leave you to work, then. I was in the middle of reading something." He turned to go, then paused in the doorway. "Feel free to pick a wine to go with whatever you're making. There's red and white in the pantry—well, you saw. I'm not saving any of it for a special occasion."

"Understood," said Nikias, trying not to raise his eyebrows.

Kallion left, and Nikias turned back to the ingredients piled on the counter and realized he was absurdly nervous. He had planned to cook something he had made many times in his master's home, a simple dish that he was confident he could make well. He'd bought the expensive cheese and the pepper thinking to fancy it up a bit for Kallion's cosmopolitan tastes, to detract from the fact that he was using salt fish—he was a little bit ashamed about that, here on the coast. Kallion's comment about choosing wine had thrown him, though, and he tried to convince himself that after all this was *really* just about enjoying the kitchen, wasn't it?

He busied himself with the meal. He soaked the salt fish, grated cheese, tore up greens, mixed dressing, beat eggs, built up two small fires on the stovetop, and set about cooking. When everything was almost ready, he opened the pantry door and looked at Kallion's wine collection.

He knew he wanted a white to go with the meal, but beyond that, he had no idea what the cryptic marks and initials on the clay bottles meant, and he selected one at random, thinking it looked like neither the most expensive nor the cheapest—though really, he had no idea. His master had only ever kept one kind of wine in his cellar.

He unstoppered the bottle and filled a jug from the kitchen shelf. Then he took two cups—the only two cups— down and headed for the dining room. He was halfway there when he realized how strange and unprecedented it was that he should have automatically taken down two cups, and one of them was for him. It was the first time he had cooked a meal that he was going to sit down and eat with someone else.

Delicious smells had been drifting out from the kitchen to where Kallion sat trying to read in his front room for some time before Nikias emerged with a jug of wine and two cups. Kallion was relieved to see that there were two cups. He'd never had anyone cook dinner for him—just him—and he had begun to worry that Nikias might try to put his food down and go back to the kitchen, not intending to eat with him. Which would be very odd—but then, it seemed odd to Kallion that anyone should want to cook in the first place.

He got up from his chair, putting down the documents he hadn't been reading. "Dinner's ready?"

"Just about."

Kallion watched Nikias putting down the cups and filling them, something else no one had ever done for him at his own table.

"I should change," he said vaguely. He realized he was not dressed in any way that he would have thought appropriate to receive guests—but then, he never received guests.

Nikias looked up. "Oh, come on. You're fine."

Of course Nikias was not dressed like a guest; he was dressed, as usual, like what he was, a working man.

"I'll help bring out the food," said Kallion, and headed for the kitchen before Nikias could tell him not to. He picked up a bowl full of salad greens.

"Thanks," said Nikias, and picked up the remaining dishes, balancing them with a practiced air.

They arranged everything on the table and sat down. Kallion reclined automatically, a habit he'd been trained in from childhood in his master's house, but Nikias just toed off his sandals and tucked up his legs. Kallion picked up one of the cups and inspected the wine, curious to see what Nikias had chosen. It was a white, and from the distinct aroma of pine resin, it had to be the Rhostian white that Epaphras had given him in the summer. That was a more interesting choice than he had expected. People either loved Rhostian wine or they hated it.

"It's fish cakes," said Nikias, gesturing to the dishes. "And there's salad and bread."

There were three dishes on the table: the simple dressed salad, the triangles of fresh bread, and the heap of small, crisp, fried fish cakes, with a smaller bowl—one Kallion didn't recognize as belonging to him—filled with sauce.

"It looks delicious," said Kallion.

It did look delicious, but not like something you would cook for someone you were trying to impress, which made Kallion feel—was it relief? Or disappointment?

He took a piece of bread, folded it around a fish cake, dipped it in the sauce, and took a bite. He changed his mind. The flavour was sophisticated; the sauce was sweet and spicy with pepper, and there was some kind of sharp cheese in the cakes.

"This is—" He had to make an effort not to praise it with his mouth still full. "This is splendid. Did you make this up?"

"No, no. It's something I used to cook all the time at home. Well, not exactly like this. I did make up the sauce. You like it?" He looked pleased.

Kallion nodded, busy eating again. He tried the salad, which was as simple as it looked, but that just showed that Nikias knew when less was more.

"It's a nice kitchen," said Nikias, taking a fish cake for himself. "Good light and ventilation, and I can't get over the running water. In my building, the apartments on the ground floor have kitchens and baths, but nobody above them does. I don't think I've ever heard of anybody having running water on the third floor."

"It's not that common," said Kallion, though in fact he had no idea. He hadn't exactly been inside many apartments in Pheme.

Nikias reached for his wine cup and took a drink. Then he held the cup away with a startled look.

"I'm sorry, I think there's something wrong with this wine." He looked up with alarm at Kallion. "You're not drinking it, are you? I just chose it at random. I think it must've … " He looked embarrassed to continue, to accuse Kallion of having spoiled wine in his cellar.

Kallion took a deliberate swallow from his cup. "It's Rhostian white. It's resinated. It's supposed to taste like this. Goes beautifully with the fish cakes."

"Oh."

Nikias now looked so much more embarrassed that Kallion really tried hard not to laugh—but he couldn't manage it at all, and had to bury his face in the crook of his arm for a moment to bring his amusement under control. When he looked up, to his relief, Nikias was smiling.

"I'll open something else for you, shall I?" Kallion suggested, moving to get up.

"No, don't do that! If it's really supposed to taste like this ... " Nikias took another sip from his cup. "It's not *bad* —it's interesting."

"If you're sure ... "

Nikias underlined his certainty by taking quite a large swig of the wine. Kallion found himself suddenly for a moment hypnotized by the picture he presented sitting there on the other side of the small table, with one leg folded under him and the other knee drawn up, the skirt of his short tunic revealing a lot of light brown thigh. He was like his cooking, Kallion thought: he seemed straightforward and unsophisticated, but he was full of hidden complexity. It made Kallion want to know more, much more.

He was eating his fourth or fifth fish cake when Nikias said, "If you were born in Photis's household, are your mother and father still there?"

Kallion shook his head. "My mother died ten years ago, just after Old Photis." He paused, reached for another piece of bread. "Who was probably my father, all things considered. Though I don't know—my mother never said that he was."

"Oh," said Nikias, and he looked like the idea of the master of the house having bastard children with his female slaves wasn't as unremarkable to him as it was to Kallion and, realistically, the entire rest of the world. "I wonder if that was why he had you brought up so fancy."

"Fancy?" Kallion repeated, amused.

"Yeah, you know. Reading and writing and not knowing how to cook and liking weird pine-needle wine. Fancy."

"He had a lot of fancy slaves, though."

"I heard that. He used to enter you into contests?"

"Yes. I was the orator—I won prizes as a youth, and might have won more if slaves had been eligible to enter all the contests."

"Were you grateful to him?"

"What, for the education? Well … yes, I suppose. I'd have rather been a chariot driver, as a boy, but you couldn't dream about things like that—well, you know how it is. And I was grateful not to have to do any of the heavy work around the house—I remembered to be grateful for that, because my mother always reminded me. But when your whole purpose is being good at your studies and winning prizes for your master … " He wasn't sure how to finish the sentence. These were things he had never articulated before. "You worry what will happen to you if you stop winning."

Nikias looked up at him through his lashes. "Like a racehorse or something."

"Yes, exactly like that."

"Do you want dessert?"

"What? Oh, there's dessert?"

"It's in the kitchen."

Kallion knocked back the last of his cup of wine and got to his feet. He picked up the dish that had contained the fish cakes. "I'll open another bottle—something you'll like."

# CHAPTER 10

DESSERT WAS CUSTARD, which Nikias had left cooling in individual moulds (borrowed from Pyke) in the kitchen. To his satisfaction, both unmoulded perfectly when he turned them out into bowls. He poured warm honey over them while Kallion broached the new bottle of wine he had brought out from the pantry and refilled their cups. They ate in the kitchen, Kallion perched on the counter, Nikias leaning against the sink.

"So … writing contracts for people, is that what you spend most of your time doing?"

"Most of it, yes. I'm studying the law texts in the hope that I'll be able to work as a jurist eventually."

"You don't want to be an advocate? Stand up in court and defend people? I'd have thought you'd be good at that."

"I would. I have the training. I don't want to do it."

"Got it." And he did. It had probably been a stupid question.

"This is delicious custard," Kallion said, changing the subject.

"I'm glad. You were right about the wine—I do like it."

"It's Pyrian, like you." Kallion looked embarrassed. "Though that's not actually why I thought you'd like it."

Nikias laughed. "Sure it is! Pyrian wine is what you bring out at the end of the party when everyone's too far gone to tell what they're drinking. Even I know that."

"Ah—most Pyrian wine is indeed pretty insipid, but *this* is from the Skodatis Mountain, and they only make it after an exceptionally cold autumn, when the grapes have frozen on the vine. That's what makes it so sweet." Kallion ran his spoon carefully around the inside of his dish, scraping up the last of the custard and honey, and licked it thoroughly. "Shall we go out and sit on the balcony? It won't stay warm enough to sit out for long, but … "

"Good idea!" Nikias put his bowl in the sink. "Should I get chairs?"

"There's one out there already."

Of course there was *one*. Nikias was getting the idea that he wasn't just the first person to cook in Kallion's kitchen but maybe the first—certainly one of the first—to visit his apartment at all. And it looked lived-in, like Kallion had been moved in for a while.

Nikias fetched a chair from the atrium, and Kallion opened the shutters onto the balcony.

The sun was setting spectacularly into the harbour. Nikias whistled appreciatively. He had been expecting another woodland view like the one Kallion had shown him outside the window, but of course the balcony was on the front of the building. It didn't overlook the park at all. It overlooked the city.

The Tetrina was the highest hill in Pheme, and they were almost at the top of it. The buildings in this neighbourhood were older, few more than two stories high, none blocking the sight lines from Kallion's balcony.

The balcony ran the whole width of the apartment, and there was an awning that could be pulled down to shade it. A wicker chair and a small table stood under the kitchen window.

Nikias wondered again, as he had at intervals since seeing the inside of Kallion's apartment, how a recently freed slave who worked as a clerk could afford all this.

They sat on the balcony, chairs angled toward the sunset and not quite facing each other, their cups topped up with more of the sweet, frozen-grape wine, and Kallion spontaneously started talking.

"The thing that you have to understand about my family —my household, but they always called it 'the family'—is what Old Photis was like. He was … I think people thought he was spectacular. And he was, in a way. He was completely immoral, but he managed to make everyone around him love him—worship him, almost. It's hard to explain. I suppose it was a mixture of fear and gratitude, because he was very generous, and he looked after people—but he could also be brutal. You saw that side of him more if you were one of his slaves, of course.

"He was self-made, the son of a freedman, and he was proud of it. His first business, the one he inherited from his own father, was providing security for gambling houses and brothels—not exactly illegal, though on the shady side, since of course some of those places aren't licensed. And the way Old Photis ran it, he turned it into—do you know what a protection racket is?"

"Uh … no."

"It's where you charge people to not smash up their shops, basically."

"What? Why would anybody … "

"Is everybody in the mountains this innocent, or is this just you?"

"I don't know if that was a real question, but of course it's not everybody in the mountains—we've got all kinds of bandits up there, but they usually just attack you on the roads and steal your stuff, maybe hold you for ransom."

"Well, think of the protection racket like holding businesses for ransom, then. You pay, you stay safe. It's all couched in this language about 'security,' as if there are other threats that they might be protecting you from—and, I mean, sometimes there are, because there are other gangsters in the city, but for the most part it's just paying not to get your place trashed by your own personal gangsters."

"I see. And this is what Old Photis did?"

"Oh, only part of it. The way he made most of his money was piracy. He wasn't a sailor at all—he outfitted a crew and remained safely on dry land himself the entire time.

"That's the origin of the Dodeki. They started with one ship and a crew of twelve. Their edge was that the ship was the best of its kind in the water, maintained like a nobleman's pleasure vessel, the crew hand-picked for their skills. They were so successful that before long they were a fleet."

Nikias took a swig of wine, feeling he needed it. "So ... the pirates aren't just friends of the family—they're employees?"

"Independent contractors, really. And they've changed a lot in recent years. Since Hesteus inherited the family business. He's—he was—a different sort of man."

"I remember Pyke telling me that, too. People sort of loved Old Photis, but they were just afraid of Hesteus."

Kallion nodded, looking out over the city for a moment. "You wouldn't have heard the old stories about the Dodeki, growing up in the mountains, but they had a reputation for gallantry. They ransomed all their prisoners and treated them well. They never sold anyone to the slave merchants. They challenged ships' captains to single combat. They rescued shipwrecked mariners—and then robbed them or ransomed them, of course, but with the utmost graciousness. At least that's what everyone said. And Old Photis encouraged all this. Insisted on it, in fact. He basked in the legend—he loved it.

"Hesteus and his father used to argue, when I was a boy, with Hesteus claiming that his father was too soft, took sentimental risks, things like that. I think he envied his father, but never understood the source of his magnetism. Almost as soon as he took over, ten years ago, there was a revolt in the Dodeki. Hesteus tried to change the terms of their profit-sharing arrangement—tried to do what he'd always thought his father should have done and bring the captains under tighter control, and four of them just took their ships and left."

"Ouch. He must have lost face over that."

"He just hired another set of men. Men Old Photis would never have chosen for the original Dodeki. He had them lay an ambush for the four defectors. It worked. They sailed right into the trap, and the new men massacred them and took back the ships, one by one. Well, except for the last one … They got away, but they were the only ones, and Hesteus's men caught up with them eventually, years later, and brought them back into the fold.

"So that was the end of the Dodeki as gallant pirates. Now their main business is slaves—they raid all up and down the Deshan Coast and around the Pseuchaian Sea. They still have the fastest, best-maintained ships in the water. Hesteus was willing to pour money into expanding the fleet, too. They have eight ships now.

"They're not as loyal as they used to be, though. Before he died, Hesteus was vying for control with Gorgion Pandares—no, you wouldn't have heard of him. Another gangster.

"Anyway. Old Photis died when I was twelve. Hesteus kept up my education because he said I could be useful to him as a lawyer." Kallion shook his head. "I couldn't ever have been a lawyer as a slave, of course. I couldn't even have testified in court … Of course he knew that."

"What was he like as a master?" Nikias asked.

"He was … " Kallion hesitated, his expression looking oddly blank in the fading light. "He was a hard master. His first secretary tried to escape and was captured and killed. I was not happy to be chosen to replace him, and no one congratulated me."

He fell silent after that. The sun was a bright sliver on the edge of the ocean, the sky almost dark overhead. A breeze had picked up, and it was growing chilly on the balcony.

The darkness half concealing Kallion's face seemed to mirror Nikias's thoughts. He could see Kallion, but not quite. He could see that here was a man who had suffered as a slave, in ways that had shaped him, damaged him somehow, but Nikias could not yet see how.

But he didn't need to, in order to know what to say.

"I go to the radicals' meetings, sometimes," he said. "They have debates and things—you might like that."

"What?" Kallion had drawn back in his chair. "No, I don't think I would like that."

"Oh. I just thought, because of the oratory and everything … "

"No, thank you, I don't want anything to do with radicals. Not—not that I don't think you and I can be friends."

"Oh. I—" It took Nikias a moment to untangle that. "You mean you do? Think we can be friends."

"If you like. I—know we got off to a bad start, but I find you good company, and … "

"All right," said Nikias. "Friends. I can live with that."

# CHAPTER 11

"Would you yourself, while you were enslaved, have desired the abolition of slavery?" Lysandros asked, revolving his empty cup idly on its base. They were alone at his usual table in the Armoury Street wine shop.

"Well, no," said Nikias, "but I was an uneducated boy living in the mountains, and I had no personal complaints. We're talking about someone who can read and write and give speeches, who's lived all his life in the city, and says that his master was 'hard.'"

"This hypothetical man we're talking about?" Lysandros said archly.

"Yeah. Hypo for short. My point is, he's not at all what I was when I walked through these doors. He knows what this is about—and he says he doesn't want to get involved."

"He sounds like a coward."

"He is *not* a coward. I've seen him … "

"Hypothetically?"

"Oh, go away."

Lysandros groaned. "Can you at least say, 'fuck you'? It doesn't have to be fancy—you don't have to mention goats or divinities or anything."

Nikias ignored that. "My point is, I don't think this person is a coward—I don't think it's as simple as that."

"No, it rarely is. I don't suppose … " Lysandros was giving him a more serious look suddenly. "Is this the same person you were telling me about a few days ago, after the Euthalion?"

"I … may have spoken of him, yes." He hoped Lysandros didn't remember what he'd said at that time.

"You were worried about him debasing himself."

"Ye-es. But you did make me see I was in error there … I think."

"I hope so, because you were. Hm."

"Hm what?"

"Well, he sounds like a complicated individual. I wish you luck."

"With what?"

Lysandros raised his eyebrows. "With whatever you plan to do. May the gods smile upon your enterprise."

Everyone knew that Lysandros was an atheist.

"Oh, go away," said Nikias.

Nikias presented himself at the door of Satteia's house on the Rhina Hill the following morning, signed the contract in the presence of Kallion and Satteia herself, and then did not see Kallion for a week. It felt like a bit of an anticlimax.

Not that he had very much time to think about that. It was a busy week. He had shopping to do: utensils and ingredients for the new snack stand; building materials and builders to hire; a sign to get painted. He had dinner with Satteia and her husband twice—a less terrifying proposition than he had expected, because her house was much less grand than Old Photis's, and they were both very friendly—and discussed details of the business. He consented to have his name painted on the sign, though he had been inclined to want just pictures of snacks, because Satteia said that in the Tetrina market everyone had words on their signs. A surprising number of people in the city could read these days, she said. He planned out a menu, tested a couple of new ideas in Pyke's kitchen, toured the market, and haggled with the man in charge of rentals.

On Xereus's Day, he brought a sample from his first batch of dried sausages to Satteia's house and delivered the news that he had rented a spot in the market, and the builders would begin work in two days' time.

"Wonderful!" she exclaimed, licking her fingers. They were sitting in her garden, which had so many statues of animals in it as to seem eccentric. "Do you need more money?"

"No, I have money left over. I'll go get it changed into small coins for the float—that's what you call the money you keep on hand to make change for people—and I should be all set to open."

"Excited?"

"How could you tell?" He beamed.

He really liked her. She was a rich, beautiful woman who somehow had no air of superiority about her at all. Or maybe it would be more accurate to say that her superiority was so total, so effortless, that it didn't bother him.

"The twentieth is a propitious day to open," she said. "I spoke to my astrologer friend. Do you think you'll be ready by then?"

"The twentieth of this month?" Nikias tried to remember what day of the month it was today. "I should be."

"Excellent! Invite your friends, so you're sure to have a crowd. That always attracts people to try out a new place."

"My friends are mostly radicals—I don't know how well they behave in crowds," Nikias said.

He was joking, of course. He would invite Lysandros and

the others from Armoury Street. Lysandros might bring some of his students from the Marble Porches, too.

But Satteia was giving him an intrigued look. "Radicals, really? You didn't seem to me the type—which just goes to show that I don't know anything about it."

"Well, I don't get up and speak at meetings."

"No? But what do they say? When they do get up and speak."

And so, with a feeling as if this couldn't be quite real, Nikias found himself explaining some of the arguments of the radicals to Satteia in her statue-filled garden. She listened with interest.

"So what you need, at this point," she said musingly, "is more people to free their slaves and show everyone how well they are able to go on afterward. Is that right?"

"That's right. We have the example of Tios, where they freed all the publicly owned slaves first and then went on to outlaw slavery for private citizens, but everyone says, 'Oh, that's the colonies, it wouldn't work in Pheme.' And they're sort of right—I mean, it's clear we can't do it the way Tios did, from the top down. We have to start from the bottom up. Er—no, that's not quite what I mean."

"Yes, because 'from the bottom up' would mean slave revolts, wouldn't it?"

"This is why I don't get up and speak at the meetings." Even sounding accidentally like you might have been encouraging a slave revolt could get you into very serious trouble.

"Well, you've convinced me," said Satteia simply.

Nikias stared at her. "I've … "

Oh. She was joking. She had to be.

She laughed. "I was being disingenuous when I said I didn't know *anything* about it. Some of my friends have freed their slaves—Agathe Timone and Nione Kukara? Maybe you've heard of them. Both former Maidens of the Sacred

Loom. But you really are the first person to explain to me the arguments for it. I suppose I was waiting to be convinced."

Nikias sat just thinking about that for a few moments. He thought about the slaves he had met at the Euthalion party who belonged to Epaphras's household. Tiko, whom he had been trying not to think about at all since that night—he hadn't seemed to expect ever to be freed, but would he be, now, because Nikias had had a conversation with his master's wife? Itia—would she be freed?

"Would you want to free the slaves at—at your brother-in-law's house too?" he blurted.

She didn't appear to find the question rude. "I'll talk to Epaphras about it. They're technically his, now, I suppose. Though I wish we had some assurance that Hesteus wasn't going to pop back up to claim everything one of these days."

Nikias felt cold. "You think he might?"

She spread her hands. "They never found his body. He's *probably* dead, but for me that's not good enough. People like him don't die when you want them to."

"How did he ... I mean, how do they think he died?"

"By violence." She made a face. "There was a blood-stained cloak, or some such, and signs that his body had been dragged to a river door—it happened in one of those houses that backs onto the river—and dumped in the water. But nobody actually saw him die. What they saw was him go into a house to meet some people and never come out."

"Who saw it?"

"Relatively trustworthy people, I'm told. Some of his own men who were waiting for him, and some neighbours. Of course the murderers, or whatever they were, got away. They were some of his own men, too, or so Epaphras thinks."

"But it could have been ... what? Staged? He might not have been dead when he went into the river?"

"Either on purpose or accidentally. The court ruled that

he was dead and Epaphras could inherit, but of course if Hesteus turns up alive, that won't matter."

Nikias remembered the flat, emotionless way Kallion had said, "He was a hard master." He remembered the certainty he had felt that Kallion had been damaged in some way he could not quite grasp.

"Immortal gods," he murmured.

The next time Nikias went to meet with Satteia and her husband, they were at Epaphras's father's house, so he walked back to the familiar neighbourhood of Pyke's Snacks, saw the deserted stand with the sign taken down, and revisited the scene of the disastrous Euthalion party. Kallion was in the atrium. He was standing politely in the background as Elpis and Rhoias argued with each other from opposite sides of the rain-water pool.

"Our father always wanted to be a great man," Elpis was saying. "He wanted the world to look up to him."

"Then maybe he shouldn't have—"

"Be quiet, I'm talking. He wanted that, but he never achieved it. My brother Hesteus was on the verge of achieving it when he was tragically taken from us. You should know that. I felt I should tell you. He would have been a great man in the eyes of the world."

Rhoias was white-faced and almost shaking. It looked like rage rather than fear. "He didn't want 'the eyes of the world,' you—you harpy. He just wanted to rule his little kingdom like a tyrant."

Elpis gaped. "How dare you? You don't know how hard it was for him, the disrespect he endured. From his slaves, from his fellow citizens—even from you! You don't know what he had planned and what he would have achieved, if it hadn't been for—"

She broke off as she noticed Nikias.

"What is *he* doing here?" Elpis demanded.

"I've brought cheese balls for Mistress Satteia," Nikias said, holding up his basket.

"Here, I'll take you to her," said Kallion, springing into action. "I'm surprised we haven't run into each other before now," he said in the colonnade, smiling.

"I've been so busy this last week. There's so much to *do*, when it's your own business. You've no idea—well, I don't mean that, exactly. You probably do have some idea." He grinned.

"Are you … having fun, though?" Kallion spoke as if the concept was slightly foreign to him.

"Tremendous fun. I've got a spot in the market picked out and paid for, the builders come tomorrow, and if all goes well I should be able to open the Xereus's Day after next."

"That's wonderful! We should … if you want to, do something to celebrate. You should come over, and I'll find another wine you'll like. I don't have any more of the Skodatis Mountain ice wine, I'm afraid, but … "

"You mean I should come over and cook dinner for you again."

"No, of course not. You have enough to do—enough cooking to do, too."

"Well, actually, I was thinking of asking if I could use your kitchen to test out a couple of new recipes."

"Oh, of course! I was thinking of that, but I forgot. How have you been managing without a kitchen?"

"I've been doing stuff over at Pyke's—she's been a big help. But it's crowded over there. Pyke and her sister and her niece all need to cook for their family, and I'm in the way more often than not. It would be bliss to be the only person in the kitchen for a change."

"Come over whenever you like. Well—whenever I'm at

home, which I usually am in the evenings. Come over tonight."

"All right," said Nikias with a grin. "I will."



"I'm going to try to make these dumplings that my master's second wife used to cook," Nikias said, setting down his bundle of ingredients and his pot and rolling pin. "I've never cooked them before, so this may end in tears. And they're more sweets than dinner."

"I'll go down to a cookshop if we need something more to eat. Can I watch?"

"Sure. Hey, where did these come from?" He was looking at the small stack of bowls and cooking utensils in the corner of the work surface.

"Oh, I bought them," Kallion said, as breezily as he could. "I thought I ought to have a few more things in the kitchen."

In fact, he'd gone out and picked out the bowls the day after Nikias came to his apartment the first time, and over the following week, after seeking advice from several different vendors and the cook at Epaphras's house, added a couple of knives, a mortar and pestle, a frying pan, and some spoons. If Nikias hadn't wanted to come back and use his kitchen again, he didn't know what he would have done with it all.

"That's a good knife," said Nikias appreciatively, weighing the larger of the two knives in his hand and inspecting its edge.

Kallion was pleased. He leaned against the counter and watched Nikias begin setting out ingredients and mixing dough. Occasionally Nikias would ask him for something— "Hand me the raisins, will you?"—and Kallion felt he managed not to be an actual impediment in the cooking process. At some point he realized he had started asking questions.

"Won't it fall apart if you roll it out so thin?"

Nikias gave him a tolerant look. "Hopefully not."

"Sorry, sorry. Er, is there anything I can do to help?"

"Well … " Nikias glanced behind him at the stove, then back at the rolled-out dough and the bowl of filling on the counter. "How about you start filling them while I build the fire and get the water boiling? Don't look so alarmed—I'll show you exactly what to do."

So Kallion found himself scooping spoonfuls of wine-soaked raisins and grated cheese and making precise little piles on the dumpling dough that Nikias had rolled out. It took him much longer to finish this job than it took Nikias to make the fire and put the water on the stove, so Nikias ended up back on Kallion's side of the kitchen, watching over his shoulder.

"You really never had to work in a kitchen, did you?"

"Am I doing it that badly?"

"No, no. I just meant—well, I suppose everyone at my master's house knew how to do most things that needed doing on the estate. He had a cook, but when she needed help, she'd just call in whoever was around. And of course if you wanted food when she was busy or out or gone to bed or something, you had to know how to make it for yourself."

"I think your master's household was unusually casual," said Kallion. This wasn't a conversation he particularly wanted to have. "Most big households in the city have specialized staff."

"We weren't really a big household—although my master was an aristocrat."

"Was he a good master?" Kallion asked, for something to say.

"I would have said so at the time."

"But now?"

"Now I would say there's no such thing."

"Ah." Now that was a conversation Kallion *really* didn't want to have. "All right, I've finished. What do we do next?"

There was another lump of dough to be rolled out, which Nikias laid over the sheet with the piles of filling, sealing it down and then cutting it up into neat little square packets, which he expertly tipped into the boiling water. They came out steaming and fragrant, and Kallion and Nikias each ate a big bowl of them and didn't need anything else for dinner.

# CHAPTER 12

"Stamos and I and some others are going to the races tomorrow, Nikias," said Ora, the wife of one of his friends at Armoury Street. "Do you want to come?"

Nikias sighed. "I guess so." He poured himself another cup of wine. "I won't be able to get much work done on a race day anyway."

The construction of the market stall had been delayed, and it wasn't going to be ready until the 24$^{th}$ of the month now. The builders wouldn't be working on race day, the vendors from whom he needed to buy things wouldn't be working, the market would be shut, and Pyke and Satteia and Epaphras would probably all be at the races themselves, so he wouldn't even be able to plan anything or test out any recipes. And as for Kallion …

"Well, don't sound so excited about it," Ora retorted. "You can't work all the time, Nikias."

"I like working," he said, a little sourly. "I like making food and serving it to people. I want to get *back* to work. Because I also like making money and taking it home at the end of the day. I don't see anything wrong with that."

"You're grumpy tonight," Ora observed, but with a hint of sympathy.

"I guess so," he said. "Sorry."

He hadn't seen Kallion in a couple of days. The previous evening, deciding to take matters into his own hands, he had bought a fish, asked Pyke's advice about how to cook it, and gone to Kallion's apartment. Kallion had not been at home. Nikias had sat on the front steps of the building for a while, watching the sunset, but Kallion had not returned.

Finally, hungry and dejected and worried that the fish would spoil, he'd gone down to a place in Lower Goulina where he knew sailors and dockhands gathered in the evenings around communal cooking fires, shared the fish with some newfound friends, and drank more than he needed of the cheap wine they offered him in return. It wouldn't have been a bad evening, actually, if he'd intended to spend it that way.

The sailors teased him about getting stood up with his expensive fish—it was immediately obvious that was what had happened—and suggested offerings his woman might have liked better. He tried to imagine waiting on Kallion's front steps with an enamel bracelet or a shell hair-comb. He wondered whether Kallion would have laughed or looked alarmed. It would have been one of the two.

He ran into Pyke, with her sister and niece and several of her niece's children, outside the Hippodrome the following morning. It was a cold morning, and everyone was wrapped up in cloaks and mantles. Pyke and her family were dressed in their smartest clothes, with bracelets and dangling earrings and decorative pins stuck in their hair. Nikias felt shabby in his workday tunic and plain homespun cloak. He hadn't even put in the fancier of his two pairs of earrings.

"I haven't been to the races before," he admitted.

"What, never?" Pyke's sister gaped at him.

"Nikias only came to the city in the spring of this year," said Pyke. "And he's been hard at work ever since," she added approvingly.

"Oh, you're new to Pheme," said Pyke's sister, and then began asking Nikias about life on Pyria as they queued to enter the building.

"He didn't come from Pyria last spring," Pyke corrected her. "He lived on an estate in the mountains."

Pyke's sister seemed to lose interest in him at this point, but Nikias spotted the people he was supposed to be meeting and excused himself. Ora and Stamos had come with Lysandros and a couple of other Armoury Street regulars, Agapios and Kore, a pair who always showed up together, in elegant clothes, but were apparently not a couple. Lysandros was dressed as he always dressed, in a plain mantle, just on the respectable side of grubby, wrapped as though he had slept under it and just got up. Nikias had begun to think of it as his philosopher's uniform.

They had arrived early and got good seats, or so Nikias understood from the way everyone else talked about where they were sitting. They were on the curve at the far end of the track, down near the front, with a good view of the finish line.

"To get better seats than this," Ora explained, "you'd have to be a guest of the archons." She pointed to the section immediately below them, where the seats had marble backs and armrests, and a uniformed official guarded the gate.

"Hide me," said Lysandros, scooting over to tuck himself in between Nikias and Ora. "He's coming this way."

"Eurydemos?" said Kore, craning her neck. "Oh, I see him. He's with that pretty boy. I don't think you have to worry."

Lysandros shuddered in a way that didn't seem to be entirely theatrics. "You'd be surprised."

"Oh, and it looks like they *are* guests of the archons," Kore finished.

Nikias looked down at the marble-backed seats, where an older philosopher-looking type was impatiently herding an attractive, brown-haired young man toward his seat, while the young man was trying to carry on a conversation with a tall, lean, blond man accompanied by two young children.

"That's Polydoros," Ora leaned across Lysandros to whisper to Nikias, pointing behind her hand toward the blond man. "You know, *the* Polydoros."

"Maybe he doesn't know," said Lysandros dryly. "And that would be all right."

"Uh, is he the one who had to resign because of … something with an actor?"

"Yes," said Ora. "You see, he does know."

"Mm," said Lysandros.

Nikias spotted a vendor coming down the aisle selling nuts and got to his feet.

"I'm going to get a snack—can I buy for anyone else? My treat."

"We can't let you do that, Nikias," said Stamos. "We know you're not working."

"I can let him do it," said Lysandros. "See if he has hazelnuts."

"Almonds for me," said Kore. "And we'll pay you back."

Nikias turned back toward the aisle just as three people were about to sidle into the empty section of bench beside him.

"Nikias! Hello!" Satteia waved delightedly. "Look, it's Nikias."

She was with her husband and Kallion. Kallion spotted Nikias and waved too, smiling as easily as if he hadn't kept

Nikias waiting on his steps with a fish two nights earlier. But of course he didn't know he had.

He looked well. He was dressed as usual, but his clothes were always smart enough for a festival. His hair was pulled back and tied, but it was not all the same length, so some strands still fell around his face.

"Are these seats free?" Satteia was asking, gesturing to the bench beside Nikias.

"Sure, yes, er—"

"Oh, but you were getting out. Here, let's make room for you."

She and her party manoeuvred out of Nikias's way—city people were very good at this sort of thing—so that he could get past them to hail the nut-seller, and then they filed into the bench behind him. He heard Satteia greeting Lysandros as if he were an old friend, which didn't mean much since that was how she talked to basically everyone.

He bought five parcels of nuts, somewhat at random, and hoped that he wasn't going to need money for anything else for the rest of the day, because he hadn't a single obios left. Shuffling awkwardly back into their row with his hands full of greasy, fragrant paper parcels, he saw that Kallion was on the end now, so he would be sitting next to him.

"Here," said Nikias, passing Kallion all but one of the parcels. "Pass them down? I got as many as I could, but some people will have to share."

"Oh, Nikias, how thoughtful," said Satteia. "Shall we share one, darling?" she asked her husband.

Kallion had not kept a parcel of nuts for himself. Nikias opened his paper and offered it. Kallion smiled across at him as he plucked out a nut.

"Thanks. I'm glad we ran into each other."

"Yeah? Me too. I've missed you."

"Me too. I've been busy, with—" He nodded toward Epaphras beside him. "Work."

Past Satteia, Lysandros was leaning forward with his forearms on his knees to look curiously across at Kallion. When Nikias caught his eye, Lysandros gave an approving nod and straightened up to reply to something Satteia was saying. Nikias caught the word "manumission."

Down on the racetrack, a row of trumpeters marched out to blow a fanfare. The crowd cheered in response.

"I've been helping Epaphras and Satteia prepare the documents to free all the members of their households," Kallion said.

"Really?" Nikias cried. "Oh, that's—I'm so glad!"

Kallion smiled. "I knew you'd like that."

"You must be happy for everyone, too."

"Yes."

He looked—not as if he wasn't happy, exactly—but as if he was trying to be *only* happy, as if there were something he was worried about. Nikias wished he knew how to ask what it was, but maybe he would think of a way when it was a better time. Instead he offered Kallion the parcel of nuts again.

"I've never been to one of these before," he said, gesturing at the Hippodrome around them.

"No, I suppose not. I have—my first master used to bring us all the time, the whole household." He pointed down toward the track. "There's a procession before the races begin. It's pretty fun."

A line of dancers with tambourines had followed the trumpeters onto the track, and then came several ranks of athletic-looking men in long tunics which identified them as the charioteers themselves. People in the seats above were cheering and calling out the names of their favourites. The dignitaries in the reserved seats were more sedate.

"What were you saying you needed to talk to me about?" Epaphras, on the other side of Kallion, did not seem interested in the procession. "Oh, excuse me—yes, dear?" He turned back to Satteia.

After the charioteers came drummers, and then a wheeled platform, decorated with flowers and pulled by a crew of young men, carrying a statue of a young god.

"Soukos," Kallion supplied, "patron of the races."

"I knew that," said Nikias, and laughed, because he hadn't. They caught each other's eyes and smiled.

The serving archons, in their gold-trimmed mantles of office, with a trail of attendants, brought up the rear of the procession.

"Kallion," said Satteia, leaning past her husband, "Lysandros has been telling me to make sure we include … " Nikias lost the rest of the sentence, which probably wouldn't have meant much to him anyway.

The procession had reached the midpoint of the long side of the course, directly below their seats, where the finish line was marked on the ground in white. The statue of Soukos was being lifted from its platform, amid thunderous drums and trumpets and tambourines, to be placed on a stand in the central barrier, overseeing the race. The two young children of the disgraced archon Polydoros had climbed on their seats for a better view, and pointed excitedly. The brown-haired young man with the philosopher Lysandros was so anxious to avoid was also leaning forward in his seat, looking almost as delighted. The philosopher himself was slouching, arms folded, the picture of boredom.

So it really was going to happen: the household of Hesteus Photionis was going to be freed. Perhaps it wasn't the biggest household to be freed, and certainly it wasn't the most respectable, but it was the first time Nikias had been involved in such an event. He had been freed individually in his master's will, and had felt—among all the other, larger feelings he'd had at that time—slightly ashamed of it. He couldn't quite imagine what it was going to be like for the slaves of that household.

Maybe that was why Kallion didn't seem entirely happy about it himself? Maybe he had felt that sense of shame when he was the only one freed after their master's death—just like Nikias—and now he felt left out of the general excitement. But somehow that didn't seem quite right.

Lysandros would have had an answer, Nikias thought. It was probably something a lot of people felt: simple nervousness about something new. Sure, it's a good *idea* to free all the slaves, but will it really *work*?

Down on the track, the procession had made its way back to the starting gates, and the charioteers had gone in to ready their vehicles. More drums and trumpets filled up the few minutes of waiting. Even Satteia had to give up trying to have her shouted conversation. In the seats of honour, one of the archons—First Archon Hippo-something, Nikias couldn't remember his name—rose to give the starting signal, holding up a gilded olive branch. He paused dramatically, then swept the branch down, and the starting gates sprang open simultaneously, to a roar from the crowd.

# CHAPTER 13

KALLION WAS LESS interested in watching the first race than in watching Nikias watch the first race—his first race ever, which seemed special. He had come to the Hippodrome anxious to have a conversation with Epaphras and thinking that they would have plenty of time to talk, as he knew his patron was not at all interested in the races himself. Now he wished that Satteia's enthusiasm were more infectious, or that she didn't have her new friends the radicals to share it with, so that she could have distracted more of her husband's attention.

"You said it was something to do with ships," Epaphras prompted him.

The green-and-white chariot was already leading the pack on the first lap, and Polydoros's children were bouncing in their seats and cheering. Of course—that was their father's team. Kallion wanted to point this out to Nikias, who was completely absorbed in the spectacle, sitting forward and gripping the edge of the rail in front of them with both hands.

"Ships," Kallion forced himself to say instead. "Yes. The ships you asked me to try to sell."

"The … " Epaphras looked blank for a moment. "Oh, yes. The ships at Oxos. Have you been able to find buyers?"

"No, because the ships seem to be—"

"Darling, look!" Satteia tugged her husband's arm excitedly, and his attention was instantly diverted from Kallion.

At that moment, the purple-and-gold team took the turn at the far end too tightly and capsized in a tangle of writhing limbs and snarled traces. Nikias gasped. Attendants from the barrier ran forward to drag the charioteer free, others to deal with the horses. The charioteer was bleeding, but able to walk, and to wave ruefully at his groaning supporters in the stands. The horses were cut free from the traces and led limping away. Meanwhile, the stragglers on the course swerved as they thundered around the wreck, and green-and-white pulled further into the lead as the attendants lowered the first flag on the barrier to mark the beginning of the race's second lap.

"He's all right," Nikias breathed, not taking his eyes off the course. "Divine Anaxe be blessed. But the poor horses! I see why I've always heard this was a dangerous sport. He was lucky, wasn't he?"

"He was smart," said Kallion, leaning forward in his seat so Nikias would hear him without having to turn. The crowd behind them was very loud. "You see how some of the drivers wrap the reins around their waists? It's a new technique, lets them lean their whole body weight into their turns. But—"

Nikias had put a hand to his mouth, staring out at the track in horror as he saw the implication of what Kallion was describing. "They could be dragged to their deaths!"

"Yes," said Kallion, wishing he hadn't brought it up. It wasn't a hypothetical matter. Some charioteers had been killed that way; Kallion had seen it himself. He couldn't imagine how Nikias would have reacted to that. "The race committee has been talking about banning the practice," he said, trying to sound reassuring.

"Sorry, you were saying?" said Epaphras.

"Right." He couldn't remember what he had been saying.

"Green-and-white's not got his reins around his waist," Nikias reported.

Polydoros's team was undefeated for the last two years; his charioteer was reputed to have magical powers and was the subject of countless stories.

"I'm glad," Nikias said, still fixated on the race, where the red team was making a break from the pack. "Wouldn't want those kids to see him come to harm, you know?"

What a sweet thing to say. Kallion wanted to give Nikias a hug. He'd remembered what he had been about to tell Epaphras about the ships, though.

"They're gone."

"Eh?" said Epaphras. "What's gone?"

"The ships." He was still getting a blank look, so he elaborated: "The ships that your brother purchased at Oxos before his death, which you told me to sell. They appear to be gone."

"That's good, isn't it? No, no, I do see it's actually quite bad. Er, any idea what's happened to them?"

"No idea, sir." It wasn't quite true. He did have an idea, but it made him feel so sick with terror he couldn't bear to mention it. He'd been avoiding thinking about it.

Even if he could have said it, he wouldn't have been heard just then over a huge, groaning roar from the crowd. Even Nikias had made a noise.

"Are they allowed to do that?" he asked, turning to appeal to Kallion.

Kallion looked down at the track. He had, of course, missed what had happened, but he could see the aftermath. There had been another crash, at the end of the third lap, and the blue chariot lay smashed against the barrier while attendants scrambled to free the thrashing horses and cut the unconscious driver loose.

"The yellow team pushed him against the barrier on purpose," Nikias explained. "At least it looked on purpose."

"He could get suspended, if the judges agree with you," said Kallion. "They're not allowed to do that—but it's hard to do anything about it. And they always claim it was an accident."

It was a race between red and green-and-white now, both so far ahead of the rest of the pack that it seemed unlikely anyone else would catch up. But there were four laps to go, and that left plenty of time for things to change.

"You didn't hear me, did you?"

Kallion sat up sharply, embarrassed. "No, sir, I'm afraid I was distracted. What did you say?"

"Is it possible Hesteus sold the ships just before he died, and it didn't make it into his records?"

"Well … I kept his records, and I'd never heard about it. But you're right, it could very well be a misunderstanding of that kind."

"But you think they might have been stolen?"

The yellow driver was whipping his horses frantically and drawing up behind green-and-white, and Nikias was shouting along with Polydoros's children and whoever's decorative boyfriend that was in the archon's seats. The ships at Oxos seemed like the least important thing in the world.

"They were … claimed by someone."

"They *what*?" Epaphras cupped a hand around his ear.

Red was drifting to the side, losing ground in his attempt to stay clear of yellow, who was gaining on green-and-white now, heading into the fifth lap.

"Claimed!"

"Flamed? What?"

Red had dropped out of the running, and it was yellow against green-and-white now. Satteia and the radicals were shouting too by this time. Green-and-white took the treacherous turn at the far end with ease, and now there was only one flag left on the barrier, and they were into the final lap.

"Someone took them! The ships!"

"Yes, yes!" Epaphras nodded enthusiastically. "Stolen! That's what I was saying!"

Nikias reached out and gripped Kallion's arm. The villain in the yellow chariot made an obvious attempt to drive green-and-white against the barrier on the nearer turn, but green-and-white put on an astonishing burst of speed, as if his horses had been taking it easy through the rest of the race, avoided yellow by a hairs-breadth, and went streaking on toward the finish line.

"That's all right then! Kallion?"

"Sir?" Kallion could not take his eyes off the track, not even to show respect to his patron.

"Come on, come on," Nikias cried. His hand had found Kallion's, and they were holding on tight.

"I said that's all right, it's—"

"Epi, darling, let him watch the race with his boyfriend." Then Satteia shrieked. "Blessed Soukos, look at that!"

Yellow was lashing his horses like a madman, but they would have needed wings to catch up to green-and-white. Red hadn't given up after all, and plunged into the newly opened space on the track to edge past yellow and pull into second place. Green-and-white was across the finish line and cantering easily to a halt while the crowd screamed and whooped. Nikias was on his feet, and so, to his own surprise, was Kallion. Nikias glanced at him and grinned.

"This is much more fun than I expected," he admitted, in between cheers.

"I know! I never had this much fun before."

They were still holding hands, and let go reluctantly.

"I'm terribly sorry, sir," said Kallion, turning toward Epaphras.

"No, I'm sorry. I should have let you watch the race,

Satteia is right. I didn't realize … " He gestured vaguely toward Nikias. "Carry on."

The races went on all morning. None of them was quite as gripping as the first, but to Nikias, sitting next to Kallion, exchanging smiles, picking favourites among the teams, and occasionally holding hands as the chariots neared the finish line, it was all thrilling. Satteia sent Nikias to buy more snacks, so he and Kallion shared a shrimp pastry, which was disappointingly soggy, and Nikias critiqued the cook's technique.

Polydoros's children began to get restless during the third race, and their father took them out after it was over. The philosopher in the archon's section quarrelled with his boyfriend at around the same time and tried to leave in a huff, came back, quarrelled some more, and finally left with the boyfriend trailing glumly behind him. Epaphras stopped trying to talk to Kallion and just enjoyed his wife's company.

Nikias tried not to hear the familiar voice in his mind, calling the races "the worst excess of the decadent city," deploring the way they encouraged idleness and gambling among the common people. Well, he was common, and here and now he was free to be common and enjoy common things if he wanted to. And, it turned out, he did.

So did Kallion, for that matter. Kallion had even jumped up and cheered with him at the end of that first race. Nikias had been unreasonably pleased about that.

After the last race, the crowd poured out of the Hippodrome to enjoy the rest of the day off, or to go back to work if they were so unlucky. Nikias and Kallion were next to each other in the press of people leaving, but separated from the rest of their party. Holding hands now was simply a practical necessity.

"Do you want—" Nikias started.

"I'm afraid—oh, sorry. What were you going to say?"

"No, you first."

"Well, I'm afraid I've got to go somewhere for lunch. Otherwise … "

"Right. With Epaphras and Satteia?" Nikias asked, thinking he could probably invite himself along.

"No, sadly. Or I'd invite you. We've sort of got the same patrons now, don't we? Or, at least, a matched set." Kallion smiled.

Nikias smiled back. "Well, I was going to invite you for lunch, just so you know."

"I know. But I have to see a client."

The crowd had thinned, and they let go of each other's hands.

"I understand," said Nikias, because of course he did.

"Look, I think that's Widow Pyke waving to you," said Kallion, pointing. "Well—I'll see you."

"Yes. Soon—I'll see you soon."

"I had a good time!"

"Me too."

"I know."

Pyke overtook Nikias as he stood watching Kallion walking away.

"Was that Hesteus Photionis's secretary you were talking to?" she asked in surprise.

"No, that handsome young man?" said Pyke's sister in astonishment. "How chilling!"

Nikias gave her a more annoyed look than he intended and immediately felt bad for it.

"I just meant, you know," she said, "you expect to be able to see it in people's faces, don't you? The evil things they've done."

"He hasn't done any evil things," said Nikias automatically.

"Oh, he has," said Pyke, but with a quelling look at her sister. "His master was an evil man. But Kallion was his slave, and that makes a difference. I didn't know you and he were friendly."

"He helped me out at the Euthalion party, and we've—run into each other since then. We were watching the races together."

"Mm," said Pyke. "Well, you be careful. I never thought it was wise of Epaphras to keep up that connection—but I suppose he doesn't have much choice, if he wants help with the estate."

# CHAPTER 14

THE FOLLOWING EVENING, Nikias was on Kallion's doorstep again. This time he had a basket of mussels, a cabbage, and the ingredients to make a cheesecake recipe that Satteia's cook had taught him. He planned to tell Kallion that as he'd missed the expensive fish the other day, he would have to make do with mussels and cabbage today. He also planned to use some of Kallion's wine to cook the mussels and cabbage, and the results were going to be delicious and unexpectedly sophisticated. He would explain how he had helped out in Satteia's kitchen the other day specifically so he could find out how to make the cake. Of course, all of this would only work if Kallion was at home.

He wasn't. Nikias went to sit on the steps with his basket of mussels, thinking about what his friends at the docks would say when they heard about this latest failure. *Did you really think she was going to turn up for shellfish when she stood you up over bream?* He recalled their helpful suggestions about better presents and tried to picture Kallion tucking his hair back with one of the cheap carved combs that sailors bought for their girlfriends. Suddenly he realized that he could picture it very clearly, that Kallion would do it, and it would be surprisingly adorable, and why hadn't he thought to pick up one of those combs in the market? Then he could have told the whole story about the sailors and the fish …

"You look deep in thought," said Kallion, who had arrived at the foot of the stairs without Nikias noticing.

Nikias looked up. Kallion was carrying his usual satchel, with scrolls sticking out from under the flap, and wearing a mulberry-coloured mantle. His hair was tied back. It looked good like that, although of course it also looked good down.

*You expect to be able to see it in people's faces, don't you?*

Nikias cursed Pyke's sister in his head, as he had been doing all day. He didn't expect to be able to see anything in anybody's face about their character, that was nonsense, and he'd never thought just because Kallion was beautiful it must mean he was a good person. But he *was* a good person; Nikias would know by now if he was not.

"Is that for a new recipe?" Kallion asked, indicating the things on the step beside Nikias.

"No. Just—um. Dinner. If you want. It's only mussels, I'm afraid." The cheeky story he had planned to tell somehow wasn't coming readily to his lips.

"I *love* mussels. How are you going to cook them? In wine?"

"That was what I thought, but … "

"I hope you didn't buy any wine, because, as you recall, I have lots."

"I do recall."

Kallion smiled. "Good! Come on up. I'm glad to see you."

By this time Nikias's heart had thoroughly melted. "I came the other day," he admitted.

"Oh?" Kallion looked down from where he had passed Nikias on the stairs.

"Yes, two nights ago. You weren't in, but I came over with a fish that I was going to cook for you."

"A fish?"

"A bream."

"Ooh. Fancy."

"It seemed appropriate."

"Did it?" Kallion's light brown eyes were strangely intent on him. "And … what did you do with it?"

"I took it down to the docks and cooked it for some sailors."

"You *what?*"

Nikias felt his face heating up as if he'd just said something pornographic. He'd been talking about a godsdamned fish. "I shared it with some friends at the docks." It still didn't sound good. "So, you know, it didn't go to waste. The fish. They said I should probably have bought you something more suitable—jewellery or something—but between the bream and all those nuts and soggy shrimp pastry yesterday, I'm broke, so you're getting shellfish and cabbage."

"Cooked in my own wine."

"Cooked in your own wine."

Kallion shrugged. "Come on up," he said again.

Kallion watched Nikias scrubbing mussels in the sink, his big hands working under the water. The air in the kitchen felt heavy, static-charged, and the sky outside the barred window was rapidly darkening.

"It looks like a storm," Nikias said, looking up from the sink.

"Um. Yes." Of course that was what it was.

But then Nikias's eyes met his, and it was more than that, too; Kallion wasn't the only one who felt it.

"This one should work," he said, holding up the bottle of wine he had brought out from the pantry.

"Great." Nikias cleared his throat, lifting his hands dripping out of the water in the sink. He dried them on a towel that he had tucked through his belt. "Fill up that little jug there, will you?"

"Sure."

Kallion went to the counter and picked up a knife to pry up the wax seal on the bottle. Nikias was beside him, a warm presence, rolling the cabbage across the work surface and pulling off the ragged outer leaves. Thunder growled in the distance.

"That came up quick," said Nikias. He took up the bigger of Kallion's two knives and began slicing the cabbage in smooth, powerful strokes.

"Mm." Kallion held out the small jug. "Is that enough?"

"Yeah. Perfect."

Kallion tapped the stopper back into the neck of the bottle. His mouth felt dry. He didn't know what to do, how to ask for what he wanted. They had held hands at the Hippodrome, and every time their eyes had met there had been *something*—and now there was this heaviness in the air that was not just the thunderstorm. But when Kallion had tried to propose what he wanted, back on the Euthalion night, Nikias had been repulsed. He couldn't do that again; he had at least that much self-respect.

And he'd have to, because Nikias was not going to be the one to move first. He was too good. He had something that Kallion could almost have believed was purity; he was certainly inexperienced. He might still be disgusted by Kallion or what Kallion wanted. He obviously thought he *shouldn't* be, which was something, but probably not enough.

Nikias put down his knife. The cabbage lay in a pile of pale green shreds.

"We can't just stand here *looking* at each other like this," he said. His voice was rough.

"No?" Kallion was backed up against the sink. "I don't— I don't know what else we can do," he admitted in a whisper.

Nikias looked at him, standing against the opposite counter. They were only about a pace apart. Lightning flashed outside the window, and a moment later the thunder made a low, animal noise.

"Do you," said Nikias slowly, "want me at all?"

Kallion caught his breath. "Immortal gods. Yes. You're gorgeous. And I like you. But I … "

Nikias looked at him questioningly. "You what?"

"I'm not good enough for you." It sounded stupid even as he said it. He put a hand to his forehead. "That's not it. It's true, but it's not the problem."

"There's no problem," said Nikias. "At least, not the one I think you mean. I want whatever it is you want, whatever you'd like to give. But—may I kiss you, first?"

Kallion nodded, although his first instinct had been to say, *You don't have to.*

Nikias wiped his hands on his towel again, then tossed it on the counter. He crossed the space between them in a step, and he was suddenly right up against Kallion, pressing him back against the sink. He took Kallion's face between his hands and kissed him very gently.

It was so strange that Kallion almost flinched, his body reacting as if it wanted to crawl backward into the sink full of mussels to get away. But Nikias was holding him, one hand sliding up into his hair, unfastening the tie that held it, and cupping the back of his head. His other hand travelled down to Kallion's hip, and he kissed Kallion again, this kiss firm and deep. Kallion gripped the edge of the sink and let himself be lifted up so that he was perched on the edge, his thighs stretched to wrap around Nikias's thick waist.

The sink basin, which was not made to withstand this kind of thing, gave an ominous creaking noise. Kallion found himself abruptly lifted off altogether, Nikias's hands firm under his ass. He clung to Nikias's shoulders.

"You'll have to tell me how you like it," Nikias said,

looking up into Kallion's face. His dark eyes seemed all pupil. "I don't have a very … broad experience."

What did that mean? Kallion might have said the same thing himself, but he doubted Nikias meant it in the way that he would have.

The rain was coming down hard outside by this time, a fine mist blowing in at the kitchen window, and just then the sky was split with a bright flash of lightning, the thunder cracking and rolling right on top of it.

When the thunder ended, Kallion said, "If you put me down, I can show you." He tried for a sultry tone, but his voice came out sounding thin, almost desperate.

"Sorry," said Nikias, and set him on his feet. "You'll show me what you like?"

Kallion's arms were still around Nikias's neck, Nikias's hands still warm on Kallion's waist. Kallion slid down to kneel on the kitchen tiles, and he was back in familiar territory.

He waited for a moment, half sure that Nikias wasn't going to let this happen, and indeed, Nikias took a step backward. But it was only to brace himself against the counter. He tested it with his hand.

"I think this'll hold," he said. "I'm ready if you are. I've—been thinking about this a lot. What a fool I was to turn you down the first time you offered. I hope I can make it up to you."

Kallion crawled to him across the tiny space of the kitchen, ran his hands up those glorious thighs under the skirt of Nikias's tunic, and unfastened his loincloth. It unraveled on the floor, and Nikias's cock tented the fabric of his tunic, high and hard. Kallion touched it under the fabric, feeling its thickness, the soft folded skin of its head, the tangle of hair at its base. He cupped Nikias's heavy balls. Nikias spread his legs wider, leaning back on the counter.

"That's nice," he murmured. "Do you like it?"

"I love it," Kallion purred, still stroking.

Nikias's prick was huge and hot under his fingers, and Nikias was letting him take his time in leisurely exploration, as if he was happy for Kallion to enjoy this as much as he wanted.

"That's good." Nikias's eyes were half-closed, his voice rough. "I want you to—ah! I want you to love it."

Kallion lifted the fabric of Nikias's tunic finally and feasted his eyes on the dark, flushed beauty, and Nikias let him do that, too. Then he tasted: he sucked the tip, licked up the length, again and again, kissed into the wiry dark hair, nipped at the soft inside of Nikias's thighs. Nikias's moans were gentle, rhythmic, controlled; he was letting Kallion have what he wanted, carefully, effortfully. And finally:

"Can you—" Kallion's voice caught in his throat. "—put your hand on the back of my head?"

"Sure." Nikias unclenched one big hand from the edge of the counter and cupped the back of Kallion's head, as firm as before.

"Can you—push, a little?"

"Sure." Nikias's voice was so gentle.

He was gentle as he pushed into Kallion's mouth, too, gentle as he held Kallion on, using both hands now, rocking Kallion against his groin, murmuring encouragement.

"Oh, you're so good, I can't believe you're so good. Ah, Kallion, look at you just taking me like this, just taking me all the way like this, you're doing such a good job."

He came with one final thrust into Kallion's throat and gently withdrew, still holding onto Kallion, who only then noticed the tears streaming down his own face.

# CHAPTER 15

NIKIAS SLID down the counter to sit on the floor, breathing hard. The tiles were cold against his naked backside. His legs were splayed out on either side of Kallion, who knelt there neatly, his dark hair softly tumbled around his flushed face. Nikias reached out a hand and ran a thumb over Kallion's cheek, brushing away some of the tears.

He felt as if he were seeing some new vista, as if he were standing on the prow of a ship and watching the fog lift from some newly discovered harbour. He was beginning to understand something about Kallion that he could not yet put into words.

"You're so lovely," Nikias murmured, wiping Kallion's other cheek, more firmly, with his palm. "You have such a beautiful mouth." He touched Kallion's lips lightly with his fingertips.

Maybe he could really do this, Nikias thought. Be with someone—someone else. In spite of the tears, Kallion looked relaxed and happy, even sated, though Nikias didn't think he had climaxed himself. Maybe he should ask about that.

"Do you need ... you know. To come?"

Kallion shook his head minutely. "Thank you," he said hoarsely, opening his eyes. "That was—mm. That was good."

"Yeah? You're all right? I know I'm pretty big down there. My—uh—the only man who ever tried to do that to me before could never get me all the way in. He didn't think anyone could."

"Pff. Obviously an amateur."

They sat like that for a few minutes, Nikias still stroking Kallion's face and hair, Kallion leaning into his touch. The thunderstorm was receding overhead.

"Should we finish making dinner?" Nikias asked finally.

"Good idea." Kallion looked around the kitchen. "It's getting dark in here. I'll light a lamp."

It felt more than a little unreal to go back to the pile of sliced cabbage and the mussels soaking in the sink after what they had just done. Kallion was tentatively affectionate now, even playful. He leaned closer than necessary as Nikias showed him how to light a fire on the stove, and rubbed his hip against Nikias's as he fetched down a pot from an upper shelf.

"I've got to do the garlic still," said Nikias as he remembered. "I left it to last on purpose. Thought we'd better get to the, er, other business before my hands were all smelling of garlic."

Kallion laughed, and then coughed. "Really? You put down your knife when you were finished the cabbage, and you thought, 'I'd better not start on the garlic because I think Kallion wants to suck me off, and we'd better get that out of the way'?"

Nikias shrugged. "Pretty much. I'm like that. I plan ahead, you know?"

Kallion leaned in and gave Nikias a slow, plush kiss.

"Get the mussels out of the sink," said Nikias, while their lips were still close enough to touch. "Please."

In due course they were in Kallion's small dining room,

slurping garlicky braised cabbage and picking juicy mussels out of their shells. Nikias reclined to match Kallion, but on a separate couch, since Kallion had not invited him to share his. He wondered whether he should have been the one to make the invitation, or even if it should have been more than an invitation. Kallion was obviously not shy, but he did seem to like it when Nikias took charge. They finished off the rest of the bottle of wine that they had used for the cabbage and mussels.

"Have you ever had a girlfriend?" Kallion asked, out of nowhere.

"No, I've always been strictly men only. I used to think I was strange, that way—I didn't know anybody else was. I knew some men liked boys *and* women, but not men only. I didn't know very many people, in the mountains."

"I guess some people like that," said Kallion. "I mean the solitude, in places like that. But you seem to have lots of friends now, so I can't imagine it suited you."

"I can't believe I lived like that for most of my life. I wasn't unhappy—I thought I had a good life. I just didn't know … " He gestured expansively. "I didn't know all this could be a good life too."

"Was your master one of those, 'I live at my country villa for the simple life, and the city is a cesspool of blah blah blah' types?"

Nikias laughed, a little uncomfortably. "Yes, just like that."

"Not that there isn't a lot of truth in it—I mean, the city is certainly a cesspool."

"The city is great. The mountains are full of bandits and wild boars and bears and conspirators who want to over-throw the Republic and bring back the kings of Pheme."

"Who want to *what?*"

"Never mind."

"Well," said Kallion, gracefully changing the subject, "I

know you know this now, but there are plenty of men like you—I'm one. You could probably tell that."

"It's not a big surprise, no."

They talked on about various things. It was comfortable, companionable. They laughed easily and agreed about everything, not that they were discussing anything serious. They had long ago finished the food, and the wine bottle was empty. Nikias stretched out on his back, one arm flung up above his head on the couch, the other hand lying on his belly. He rubbed it idly. He felt good, full of wine and food, with a glow of satisfaction in his loins that could easily be kindled into something else.

"What do you want to do now?" he asked, looking across at Kallion. He smiled. "I brought stuff to make cheesecake, if you want. Or should we just go to bed?"

Kallion looked startled. He sat up on his couch. "You mean ... "

"I mean," said Nikias, still lying on his back and rubbing his belly, "I figured that business in the kitchen was a warm-up, and we could go somewhere more comfortable, take our time with each other. If you don't want to do it, just say—I've had a great evening already, I'll clear out if you're tired or whatever. Or if you'd rather have the cheesecake."

Kallion made a rueful noise. "It's not that. I've actually never done that."

"Done what? Had cheesecake?"

"'Gone to bed' with anyone."

"You, uh ... what?" Nikias was confused. He'd *seen* Kallion on his knees at the Euthalion party. Obviously Kallion had been with other people.

"I've sucked cocks, that's all. I've never had—the opportunity never came up. I've never done anything else."

"No kidding?"

"You have to understand, my former masters ... There

were strict rules. It wasn't safe." Kallion had begun to look agitated.

"Right," said Nikias seriously, although he actually had no idea what that could be about. He pushed himself up to sitting on the couch. "So ... what you're saying is, it's not really your thing? Or just that you don't know what you want?"

"The latter, I think. I'm sorry—I know you said you haven't had much experience, and you must have thought that I *did*, when really ... " His voice trailed off, obviously mortified. "I do, but it's only of one thing."

"Oh. No, I just meant I haven't been with many *people*. I know how to do all sorts of stuff. We could find out what you like. Together." After a moment he added, his voice low, trying for a comforting tone although he had only a vague idea of what Kallion needed comfort over, "It'd be safe. I'm safe. You know that, right?"

Kallion's eyes were bright in the lamplight. Slowly, he nodded. "Let's go to bed."

They got up from the table, leaving the dishes, which caused Nikias a bit of a pang, even under the circumstances. But his heart was singing. Ever since he had first met Kallion, he had wanted to have something to offer him, and for so long he had thought there wasn't anything. Now here it was.

"Wait," said Nikias, holding up one finger.

He ducked into the kitchen, which was dark now except for a few embers still glowing on the stove, and found the small pitcher of olive oil that he had left on the counter. Emerging, he gestured for Kallion to go ahead.

They went into Kallion's bedroom, and Nikias closed the door behind them. Kallion had brought in a taper, and he lit the lamp by the bed. Nikias put down his pitcher. It was a small room, elegant like the rest of the apartment, the bed a simple couch, but big enough for two, even when one of them was the size of Nikias. Kallion turned toward him.

"Can I see you?" Nikias asked, his voice low. "All of you."

"Of course," said Kallion, fingers tugging at his belt, suddenly uncoordinated. "Anything."

"Mm, that's rash."

"I mean it. Anything. Talk to me—like you did before."

His belt came undone and slithered to the floor, and he grabbed the hem of his tunic and yanked it up over his head. Nikias's prick, already more than a little interested, surged up to full readiness at the sight of him, lean and white, his ribs showing under his skin as he pulled the fabric up and off, his hair tumbling down to brush his shoulders. His belly was flat, his loincloth wrapped low and tight around his narrow hips.

Nikias took a step toward him. He put a hand to Kallion's throat, ran it down over his chest, slowly fingered a tight, pink nipple. Kallion shuddered.

"I never thought it could be like this," Kallion gasped. "With you—I'd've—"

"Shh," said Nikias. He brushed his fingers over the front of Kallion's loincloth. "I want to see what you've got in there. I want to look at it a bit. See if I like it."

He moved back a fraction as Kallion unfastened the loincloth and let it fall, revealing his neat, slender prick, flushed almost purple and standing out from its groomed thicket of black hair, dainty balls nestled underneath.

"Oh, that's pretty," said Nikias. "I do like it."

He moved close again, touched Kallion's shoulders, and they kissed, open-mouthed and a bit sloppy, teeth clicking against each other. Nikias had thought it was just that he'd taken Kallion by surprise the first time, but apparently Kallion really didn't know how to kiss. That was an intoxicating thought. Nikias ran his hands down Kallion's naked body.

"I might take you from behind," he murmured, cupping Kallion's tight, bare ass. "Do you think you'd like that?"

"Yes," said Kallion, eyes closed.

He lifted Kallion onto the bed and arranged him, head down, ass in the air, moving him like he was a doll, spreading his legs wide, murmuring encouragement and praise.

"Look at you, you're so beautiful, you're going to do great. You're going to take me all the way in and I'm going to come inside you again, and you're going to love it."

"I know," Kallion whispered. "I am. Please. Do it."

"Got to get you ready first." He leaned over Kallion. "You want me to undress too? You want to feel me?"

"I want to feel you, all of you."

"Mm, yeah, I want you to."

He undid his belt and pulled off his tunic. Kneeling between Kallion's spread legs, he rubbed his belly slowly against Kallion's ass, felt him quiver.

"You like that? I've got fat since I came to the city. There's so much good food." He chuckled. "Yeah, you like it, I knew you would. I see the way you look at me."

His hard dick, still trapped inside his loincloth, was bumping against Kallion's balls, and Kallion was rocking back against him, rubbing into him, moaning low, as if he would make himself come just like that.

"How do I look to you?" Kallion asked breathlessly.

Nikias paused with his hand on his loincloth, poised to undo it. "Like you're hungry," he said, his tone for a moment no longer playful. "Like you think I could fill you up. And Kallion? I can. I really can."

"You can," Kallion whispered back. "I know."

Nikias shucked off the loincloth at last and shifted around to reach down off the bed and find the pitcher of oil he had put there. He poured some into his palm, slicked his fingers liberally, and began getting Kallion ready.

He'd only been allowed to do this part himself a few times, and it had been presented as a thing you just had to get over with. But he had always secretly enjoyed it and wanted to take his time. With Kallion, he did that, not just because he wanted to but because Kallion's muscles were so tight that Nikias was afraid of hurting him otherwise. So he probed and stroked and added more oil, moving his fingers slowly. Kallion gasped and moaned and loosened up obediently.

"I think you're ready for me," Nikias murmured. "Yeah, I think you need more than just my fingers in there." He drew them out, and Kallion whimpered. Nikias put his hands on Kallion's ass and spread the cheeks gently. "You're so pretty, you know that? You're so pretty back here, all ready for me. I'm going to get inside you now," he went on, his voice dropping to the barest whisper, "I'm going to get my dick inside you, and you're going to be so good."

"Oh, please," Kallion whispered back. "Please let me be good."

"You're going to be amazing."

Nikias slicked himself for good measure and knelt up to get in position. Kallion was a different height than he was used to; the angle was different somehow. He had to rearrange them slightly before he could push in.

He did it long and slow and steady, the way he'd always wanted to but usually had not been allowed. It felt as good as he'd imagined. Kallion gave an astonished cry.

Nikias held him firmly by the hips and concentrated on moving slowly, in and out, pushing into his beautiful Kallion, taking him, filling his white body with each stroke.

He kept talking, though what he was saying was pretty much nonsense. "Don't worry, I've got you. I'm in charge, it's safe. Just feel it, just feel me, do you feel me all the way inside you? It's so good, you're making me feel so good, how do you make me feel so good?"

Kallion had pushed up onto all fours, panting and rocking back urgently against Nikias.

"Oh, honey, oh, sweetheart, I want to do this to you all night. Don't go so fast."

Instantly Kallion stilled. Nikias felt something lurch in his stomach, in a good way. He reached forward, tight inside Kallion, and petted Kallion's hair.

"Now, I'm going to pull out, and I'm going to turn you over and get your knees up and get back inside you, so I can look at your pretty face. Can you handle that?"

Kallion made a noise of assent, so Nikias shuffled back on his knees, pulling out of Kallion's body. He turned Kallion on his back and positioned him with his legs spread, his knees bent. Kallion was pliantly eager, shifting himself to give Nikias easier access. His cheeks and throat were flushed deep pink, his mouth open and wet. Nikias leaned down and kissed him deeply as he pushed inside him again.

"There you go, my honey, there you go. Do you like it still?"

"I love it," Kallion murmured.

Nikias kept it going so long that he was proud of himself. He rearranged Kallion twice more, first pulling him up onto his lap and pushing up into him, with Kallion clinging to his shoulders and tossing back his hair, then laying him down on his side and languidly finishing him off, one hand curled around Kallion's cock, stroking faster, two fingers of his other hand popped in Kallion's mouth, so Kallion could suck and lick them as he neared his climax. Nikias came first, emptying himself into Kallion's sweat-glazed, obedient body, and that sent Kallion over the edge finally, and he came with a beautiful cry.

# CHAPTER 16

BIRDS WERE SINGING outside the window, and the room was pale with early morning light. Kallion blinked around, disoriented for a moment even though he knew he was in his own bed. There was a warmth beside him—Nikias, sprawled on his back, his big chest and his soft, hairy belly rising and falling gently, like a sleeping landscape.

Kallion didn't remember inviting him to stay the night, or in fact discussing any sort of plans for what they would do after they finished making love. He thought they had just fallen asleep side by side, exhausted.

To say that it had been a spectacular night—well, that would suggest that he'd had other nights remotely like that to compare it to. It had been like a night in another world. Nikias was like someone from another world. Kallion had thought he had hidden depths, but he'd never imagined anything like that. The way he'd talked, the things he knew how to do …

Kallion sat with the sheet over his knees, looking down at the lovely man sleeping beside him, wondering what he could possibly do.

He had not meant to get into this situation. He had realized, of course, that Nikias was still attracted to him. Kallion had never stopped wanting Nikias, either, and as they spent more time together the potential for a friendship between them had become clear. But he'd thought he could keep his lust separate from his growing liking for the man; he'd thought that because their preferences were so different, it would be easy. Nikias would never take the initiative, he'd thought, because he obviously wasn't the type.

He couldn't believe how wrong he had been about that. Kallion was like some kind of fumbling amateur at sex, and it was Nikias who was a master.

He shivered as he remembered Nikias moving him on the bed last night, rearranging his limbs the way he wanted them, his big, warm hands handling Kallion as confidently as a piece of dumpling dough.

"Now be patient for me again, my honey—yes, like that, just like that, and I'll give you what you want again, and you know I want it too, so much."

So here they were. You couldn't pretend, after a night like that, that you'd just been having a good time, and it hadn't meant anything. It clearly had. Kallion felt as if he'd given up something, some piece of himself, to Nikias, and Nikias, for that matter, had probably given up something to him, because from what Nikias had said, it sounded very much as if he'd had a lover of long standing, and Kallion might be the first man, or at least one of the first men, he'd slept with since that affair ended.

Besides, even if they could have gone back to the way things were before, Kallion didn't want to, profoundly didn't want to. He wanted this to be an affair, too. He wanted Nikias to be *his* lover.

Maybe he should just let it happen. He wanted it, Nikias wanted it—Kallion was pretty sure—and maybe he should let Nikias make his own decision. Certainly that was what he should do. It was true that Nikias didn't know everything—but then, who ever really did?

Kallion reached out and lightly stroked Nikias's short hair, his broad cheekbone, the stubble along his jaw, hoping, with a desperate, tight feeling of longing in his chest, that Nikias really did want this to be a full-fledged affair.

Nikias opened his eyes, squinted in the sunlight, and shut them again. He rolled onto his side, toward Kallion, the curves of his body shifting gorgeously. The sheet, bunched up by the movement, slipped off him, exposing a thigh and the generous swell of his ass.

"I'm in your bed," he mumbled into the pillow. "It's morning—is it morning?"

"It's morning."

"G'morning, then." Nikias burrowed deeper into the pillow. His face was warm against Kallion's thigh. "Don't have anywhere to be, do you?"

"Uh. Actually, yes. I have work to do. Clients to meet. Er —well, not right now." He looked at the light coming in the window. "It's still very early."

"Mmph," said Nikias. "Good. Don't wanna get up yet."

"You're very comfortable in my bed," Kallion observed archly. "I suppose you're used to this."

That made Nikias lift his head to look up again, the expression in his dark eyes puzzled. "Used to what?"

"To … " Kallion realized he shouldn't say what he had actually been thinking, but he couldn't come up with a suitable lie. "To sleeping with someone. I suppose—you and your ex—I mean, I suppose you've had a lover, and … "

Nikias rolled onto his back again, straightening the sheet over himself. He tucked his hands under his head. He was frowning.

*Damn, Kallion, you complete ass. Why did you bring this up now?*

"Yeah," said Nikias slowly, "I can see why you'd think

that. No, I didn't have a lover, not like you're thinking. I was my master's, you know—'boyfriend' was the word we used—for four years. From the time I was eighteen until he died, which was seven months ago now. He's the only person I ever had sex with. But no, I didn't actually sleep in his bed. Immortal gods. No, never."

Kallion sat frozen. Things were falling into place finally in his mind. The man of old-fashioned virtue living in his simple house in the mountains, far from the vice of the city; Kallion knew what that sort of man thought he should want in bed, and could guess how he would feel if, in fact, he wanted something quite different.

"And that's where you learned … " Kallion forced himself to say, then let his voice trail off.

Nikias looked at him, his expression a little wry. "Yeah. He's dead, and you don't even know who he was, and I always thought it was dumb that it had to be such a big secret anyway—so, yeah. That's where I learned all that from last night. Or, that's where I figured all that out, I should say, because he sure didn't teach by example. He could barely even bring himself to describe what he wanted."

Kallion felt cold. Surely last night had been a pleasure for Nikias; surely it hadn't felt like a duty? But if it was what he used to have to do for his master … And he was a radical. He must have hated his enslavement.

Nikias tugged one hand out from under his head and patted Kallion's knee under the sheet. "It's all right," he said. "I don't mind that you asked. Probably I should have told you anyway."

"No, no. I … didn't even know what I was asking about." If he'd had a thought, it had been that Nikias might say something deprecatory about an ex-lover that would be flattering to hear.

"If you want to ask something else, go ahead." Nikias smiled encouragingly.

"Were you fond of him?" Kallion asked after a moment.

"He was my life," Nikias said simply. He broke eye contact with Kallion then and looked up at the ceiling. "I adored him. I'd never have thought to want him—it was all his idea, but once he told me, it was like my whole life lit up. I loved everything he wanted me to do to him—and I lived in torment because he *hated* it. He was so ashamed of all of it, but he kept coming back for more. He would say that he couldn't help it." He looked back at Kallion, and there was more pain in his eyes than Kallion had ever thought to see there. And yet, at the same time, he was the same calm, happy Nikias as always. "I never talked to him the way I talked to you, last night, never *anything* like that, but … sometimes I wanted to, you know? I wanted to tell him it was all right. I think it was all right?"

"Of course," said Kallion softly. "At least, I think so."

But he wasn't an old-fashioned aristocrat living in the mountains and having a pretend love-affair with his slave. So who was he to say?

"Yeah," said Nikias. "But it was his secret shame. Everyone knew I was his boy—you couldn't keep a secret like that in a household of that size, and he didn't try to—it was just the truth of how things were when we were alone together that was secret. He wanted me to let everyone see I was just doing my duty when I went with him—that was to protect *me*, because *I* would be shamed among the other slaves if they thought I enjoyed what he was supposedly doing to me. Or, I don't know—that's what he said. Probably it was because he thought they would suspect the truth if I seemed too happy. Anyway, I did exactly as he wanted, and you're the first person in the entire world I've told any of this to.

"And then," Nikias went on, looking at the ceiling again, "I came to the city, and I realized … I'd loved the wrong person." He said it without bitterness. "He'd filled my head with wrong ideas about the world, and he never freed me while he lived—because I didn't know enough to ask for it, I guess, and he didn't think I needed it."

Kallion sat silent. The only questions he could think of were ones he knew better than to ask. *Do you still miss him? Do you hate him now?* Maybe both of those things were true.

"I feel sorry for him now," Nikias said, as if it had just occurred to him. "Sorrier than I did then, because at the time I thought maybe he was right to be ashamed. But it was just nonsense. Nothing we did in bed together changed the truth of who we were to each other—you know, 'owner' and 'property.' And even still, it poisoned my mind, that nonsense— that's why … when you first offered to use your mouth on me, that time, I went on about it being debased. I should have known better—I thought I *did* know better—but somehow I couldn't help holding onto the idea that it was wrong for you to do that, to want that. I'm sorry. I should have done better."

"You don't have to be. It's … not as if you were the first person to suggest that I should be ashamed. At least you didn't say it after you'd already had me—that's what most men do."

Nikias winced. "I'm sorry."

"How did your master die?" Kallion asked after a moment. He would prefer to hear about the man's death than about his life, at this point.

"He killed himself. Remember I said there were people in the mountains conspiring to overthrow the Republic? I know about that because they used to meet at my master's house. He was one of them. He was accused of treason when someone betrayed the whole thing to the archons, and he chose to die rather than stand trial. I found out at the same time as the rest of his household—a couple of hours before, he gathered us all in the courtyard and told us to prepare the house for mourning, and how he wanted his body to be laid out when the archons' men came to arrest him."

"Nikias! I am so sorry. I am so, so sorry."

"You know, I'm all right? Thank you. I am, really. I'm so glad I came to the city, and I'm so glad I met you." He put his hand back on Kallion's knee. "I'm sorry to have had to tell you all that. I hope it doesn't … well, I'm probably not quite who you thought I was, and I'm sorry about that. But, you know, I'm also glad to have told you. Thank you for listening to all of it."

"I wish that I could do more than just listen."

Nikias laughed. He pushed himself up onto his elbows and looked Kallion in the eye. "Oh, you have, sweetheart, you have."

Kallion swallowed. "I'm glad to hear it. I'd like … to do more. Which reminds me."

He tossed back the covers and slid out of bed.

"I'll be right back," he said.

He wrapped his old blue-and-white mantle around himself and went out to his study. After a moment he returned with a tablet and stylus, and sat back down on the bed.

"What's that?" Nikias asked, sitting up by this time.

"It's my datebook. I thought we could make some plans for when to see each other. Not just, 'Come by my house some evening, and maybe I'll be in,' but whenever you and I are both free, I'll write in my datebook NIKIAS, and wherever you want me to be, and I'll be there."

An astonished smile was spreading on Nikias's face. "Really?"

"If it's what you want. It's what *I* want."

Nikias leaned in and took Kallion's face between his hands and kissed him. "My honey. My Kallion. It's what I want. You're what I want."

# CHAPTER 17

NIKIAS STOOD behind the counter of his stall in the Tetrina Market, ready to start serving his first customers. He looked around with satisfaction. The stall was bigger than Pyke's Snacks, with two vats for deep-frying, a brand-new fritter pan with a jar of batter beside it ready to be ladled in, a generous counter at the back for rolling out and stuffing dumplings, and all the tools and ingredients he needed ready at hand. Dishes of already prepared food were arranged invitingly on the front counter, and there was money in the cash box. The menu board, written out by Kallion in beautiful, clear letters, was propped next to one of the supports for the awning, and Nikias's own name was written on a banner hung across the front. There were stools along the side counters, and the stall was surrounded by small tables with more stools, for customers to sit and enjoy the food. It was more than a snack stand; it was a stylish new place in the Tetrina Market where you could stop and have lunch before you finished your shopping.

Nikias turned to his two assistants. He was glad he had asked both of them to come in this morning, because the crowd was already gathering.

"Are we ready?"

"Yes, sir!" they chorused.

"All right!" Nikias called out to the customers. "We are open for business!"

There was a cheer. It was from his friends who had come to support him for the opening, but it was nice all the same. Nikias wished Kallion were there.

He and Kallion had been seeing each other for a week now. Every morning Nikias would wake thinking about Kallion, turning over in his mind the marvellous fact that he had a lover, and every night he would go to bed thinking about Kallion too. So far he had not actually managed to spend any more of those nights, after the first, in Kallion's bed, and he was impatient for that to happen again. It would come, eventually.

True to his word, Kallion had written NIKIAS in his datebook several times, but between Nikias's obligations in the week before the opening of his market stall and Kallion's work, they had only been able to meet up during the day a couple of times, have lunch together twice, and on Orante's Day go for a walk together along a picturesque section of the old city wall near the river.

On Bread Day evening, Nikias had gone to a meeting at Armoury Street, and he had hoped that Kallion would come. Kallion had declined, though, politely but without explanation, when invited the day before, so Nikias had gone by himself. He'd wanted to show Kallion off, but he had to content himself with talking about him. Lysandros congratulated him and bought him a drink, something which was so rare that Nikias was genuinely touched.

"I hope you will be very happy," the philosopher said seriously. "And I hope he knows how lucky he is."

Nikias smiled fondly, thinking of the way Kallion looked at him these days. "Believe me, Sandy, I am the lucky one."

"Don't call me Sandy," said Lysandros.

It was a beautiful day for the opening of Nikias's stall, clear and crisp, and the Tetrina Market was busy. Kallion walked over from Court Row at noon to see how things were going. He would have liked to be there the whole day, but he had work of his own that could not be postponed.

There was a crowd around the snack stand when Kallion arrived. He recognized a couple of Nikias's friends from the Hippodrome, the curly-haired, sloppily-dressed one and the striking woman. There were several men who looked like sailors or dock-workers, probably regulars of the old snack stand, looking slightly out of place in the tony Tetrina Market. Kallion spotted Satteia, and, to his surprise, Epaphras too, munching a fritter while his wife talked animatedly with a stately-looking woman whose slave was loading up a basket with the large order she had just placed.

Nikias was busy making octopus fritters and chatting with the dock-workers across the side counter. He had two assistants; one, Kallion had been told, was Pyke's niece Oranteia, and the other was Itia.

That was another thing that had happened in the week since Kallion and Nikias first became lovers. The entire household that had once belonged to Hesteus Photionis had been freed. The house on the Shipyard Road was nearly deserted; Epaphras was putting it up for sale after he finished going through his brother's affairs. Elpis had retreated to a property on the coast which Epaphras had given her, and Rhoias had taken an apartment in Upper Goulina.

Kallion hung back from the crowd, watching Nikias work. He looked so confident and happy, in his own place, in his element. He had chosen this for himself; he might have learned to cook in his master's house, but it had been only one among many things he had been good for. Kallion wondered what it would feel like, to have that choice—not to have been trained up to be the specific thing that you were. It was pure speculation; Kallion could change careers all he liked, and it wouldn't bring him the same kind of contentment that he saw in Nikias, not now.

Nikias spotted Kallion at the back of the crowd before Kallion had a chance to come up and surprise him, which was a slight disappointment. But when Kallion did make it up to the counter, Nikias had something for him.

"Octopus fritters?" he said, offering Kallion a plate with a skewer of fresh, golden-brown fritters lying across it. "With," he added, setting a little dish on the edge of the plate, "extra sauce?"

"What do I owe you?" Kallion asked, taking the plate.

Nikias winked at him. "We'll work that out later tonight," he said, in a comically sultry tone. They both laughed.

Kallion sat at the counter and ate his octopus fritters, trying not to think too much about how he could have paid for them if Nikias had been free tonight, which he surely wasn't.

Was a week too long a time to go without sleeping with your new lover? Nikias wouldn't think he was reluctant, would he? It was just that the first time had been so astonishing, he wasn't sure how to make anything like that happen again—whether he even should. Nikias might not like to resume the role of teacher in bed; it wasn't how he related to Kallion the rest of the time, after all.

Nikias had become quite open with Kallion, not that he had ever been particularly secretive, except about the business with his master. He had talked about himself readily, telling Kallion about his life in the mountains with a frank self-understanding that Kallion could only admire. He had told Kallion that he remembered his parents slightly; he knew that they had sold him because they couldn't afford to feed all their children, and he had seemed like the one who would bring in a significant amount of money. He remembered the first time he saw his master, at the slave market on Pyria. He had many fond memories of his master's first wife, who had treated him with affection.

Nikias wasn't blind to the complexities of his situation: still mourning a master whom he had loved, but passionately committed to the cause of abolition and firm in his belief that the man he loved had wronged him. If he noticed that Kallion told him almost nothing about himself in return— well, he certainly had noticed that, he couldn't fail to, but he never said anything about it.

It was all going to change now, of course, with the market stall open and Nikias much more busy even than he had been over the last week. Kallion had been reminding himself of this. He wouldn't look up to see Nikias lounging in the doorway of the clerks' hall as he packed his satchel to leave, because Nikias would still be here, serving customers. But then he would close up the stall, and Kallion's apartment was just a couple of streets away from the market. A lot closer than Nikias's own room on the Vallina …

"So, this looks like it's been a success," Kallion remarked, looking over the full tables, when Nikias next had a moment to spare for him.

"Beyond anything I could have hoped," said Nikias, glowing. "What did you think of the fritters?"

"The best in Pheme. But they always have been. I'm so happy for you, Niki."

Nikias leaned across the counter and kissed Kallion on the cheek, letting the nickname pass without comment. He picked up a chunk of hard cheese from the counter and began to grate it. "Can I take you out to dinner tonight to celebrate?"

"What? I should take you out—but don't you have to go to dinner with Satteia and Epaphras, or … " This was what he had assumed—either that or a large party with Nikias's

radical friends, which Kallion would not want to attend—
otherwise he would have spoken sooner.

"I told them I'd be busy with you."

"You what?" Kallion was glad he had finished eating and
had nothing to choke on. "You told your patrons that you
couldn't dine with them because—"

"Because I wanted to spend the evening with my
boyfriend." Nikias said the word with adorable relish. "No, I
didn't exactly tell them that. They hadn't invited me—it just
occurred to me that they might, so I mentioned that I was
looking forward to celebrating with you." He set down the
cheese and looked up at Kallion. "I want you to know that
I'll always make time for you. It's important to me that you
know that."

"I do, and I'm so grateful." He hadn't, but he was. "Let's
go out tonight—I'll—I'll wait for you at closing time?"

"Perfect," said Nikias.

In the end, they didn't go out to dinner. They brought
leftovers from the stall back to Kallion's apartment and ate
snuggled on the same couch in his dining room. Nikias tried
not to talk entirely about himself and what a resounding
success the lunch counter had been, but Kallion didn't seem
to want to hear about anything else.

The mood had already started to shift, with Kallion
feeding Nikias and licking sauce off his fingers, when Kallion
bounced up from the couch and said, "I forgot! I got you a
present."

It was going to be earrings. Nikias's heart sank. It was an
obvious choice, because he wore earrings, but Pyrian men's
earrings were made of very specific materials in a very specific
style; it was the only connection he retained to his homeland,
a small way in which he had asserted his own identity even

during the years when he was a slave, and he wasn't prepared to compromise on it. He had been meaning to explain all this to Kallion, but it had just never come up. And now Kallion was going to give him some beautiful but inappropriate earrings, and Nikias would have to wear them, because of course he would.

"It's out on the balcony," Kallion said.

"Er, what?"

"Your present. I had them take it out onto the balcony. Come see." He picked up the lamp and beckoned.

Nikias heaved himself up from the couch and followed Kallion out the louvred doors to the balcony.

"I should have shown it to you earlier, when we still had the light," said Kallion apologetically, walking out and holding up his lamp. "But you can get the general idea."

It was a chair. Or a chair and a half: a great big, solidly-built thing with curving arms, a back, and a leather seat. It looked like something that a magistrate would sit in. Nikias laughed aloud.

"I found the carpenter who made those stools you admired in the clerks' hall," Kallion explained. "I know it's a bit gauche to give you a present that you can only use at my house, but what can I say? I wanted you to have something comfortable. Congratulations, Niki. Your business is off to a wonderful start, and that makes me so happy."

"My sweetheart," said Nikias, gathering Kallion into his arms. "Thank you. What a thoughtful present. Let's test it out."

"Um … " Kallion started to protest as Nikias grabbed the big chair by the arms and lugged it toward the door into the apartment.

"I don't want it out here right now," Nikias explained. "I want it in your bedroom."

"Why?"

"Because," Nikias said, shooting Kallion a look over his shoulder, "you still owe me for those fritters."

He put the chair in the bedroom, which was lit only by the fading daylight from the window, and sat in it, spreading his thighs a little.

"Come here," he said.

Kallion came, and Nikias pulled him onto his lap. He drew Kallion's face down, with a hand in his hair, to take his mouth in a long, exploratory kiss.

"Are you ready to learn some more about what we can do together, my lovely?" Nikias murmured against Kallion's lips. He slid his free hand up under Kallion's tunic. "Mm, seems like you are. Let's get this off for a start."

# CHAPTER 18

IN THE WEEKS THAT FOLLOWED, Nikias became a regular occupant of Kallion's bed, staying at Kallion's apartment more nights than not. Of course, Kallion reminded himself, this was in part because his apartment was so convenient—and there was the kitchen, too, and the bath, which Nikias had come to appreciate almost as much as the kitchen. And there was Kallion, whom Nikias didn't seem to have tired of yet.

Nikias didn't even seem to have tired of Kallion being needy and subservient in bed. He played his own role as if he loved it. After three weeks, he didn't have much left to teach Kallion in the way of actual varieties of sex, but he was still so much more experienced, and so comfortable taking charge, that they fell easily into the same pattern no matter what they were doing. Nikias sucking him off made Kallion feel as helpless as Nikias bending him over his desk or taking him up against the bathroom wall.

They did other things together besides making love, though they did a lot of that. Kallion went to the lending library in the Lukina and picked out a couple of novels he thought Nikias would like—*The Silver Rooster* and *Pantaleon and Leta*—and read to him in the evenings, lying with his head in Nikias's comfortable lap on the bed. When they had time, he took Nikias sightseeing in parts of Pheme that he had not yet visited.

They didn't spend every evening together, because Nikias still went out with his friends, to Armoury Street, to Pyke's house, or Satteia's. But if he said he would come to Kallion's afterward, he always did, and he always had time for something, even if it was only to cuddle on the balcony and share a drink before bed.

Kallion hadn't yet been out with Nikias's friends. Nikias had asked him once or twice, and managed to make it clear that the invitation stood without pressing it, but Kallion had always declined. It was something they would have to sort out eventually, but for now he could postpone that necessity.

It was partly, as he had told Nikias, that he didn't feel like going out with groups of people or to crowded places in the evenings. He saw and spoke to many people during the course of a day in the clerks' hall, and often after work all he wanted was to be alone—or, as it turned out, with Nikias. That was part of the explanation, and it was one that Nikias readily accepted, although Kallion thought he could tell it wasn't the whole truth.

One cold morning in the middle of Ninth Month, they snuggled in bed together waiting for the brazier which Kallion had just lit to warm the room sufficiently for them to get up. Kallion was stroking Nikias's hair, which had grown out already into tight, lush curls all over his scalp. The bottle of oil that he scrunched through them after he bathed had a permanent home on the edge of Kallion's bathtub.

Nikias ticked items off on his fingers. "So I've taught you how to cook an omelette, how to fillet a fish, how to make love in a chair … When are you going to teach me something? And what's it going to be?"

Kallion looked at him for a moment, tapping a finger on

his lips as if thinking. Actually, he'd had an answer to this question—which he hadn't expected to be asked—in mind for some time.

"I could teach you how to make a speech."

Nikias's thick eyebrows went up. "You mean, what—oratory? What would I do with that?"

"Join the debates at Armoury Street."

"Huh. Yeah, I guess that would be … " He was obviously intrigued. Kallion hadn't been sure whether he would be. "I thought you weren't, well, exactly sympathetic to the cause."

"You thought that?" Of course; what else was he to have thought? "No, that's not—I am sympathetic, of course I am."

"Right … " Nikias looked sceptical. "Because it's my thing, and you like me."

"Something like that. Anyway, I could teach you a few orator's tricks—you don't need to learn how to construct a case, or anything like that, because you'd be speaking from the heart."

Nikias chuckled. "Lysandros always says I should just get up and speak regardless. He thinks I'm very persuasive."

"You convinced Satteia to free her household, didn't you?"

"Nah, she just pretended I convinced her—I think she was basically convinced already." After a moment he said, "But I like the oratory idea. How do we start?"

"It's not going to be as much fun as the things you've taught me … "

Nikias rolled his eyes. "Yeah, well, I can't help it if I'm the one of us who knows all the fun stuff."

So after that, of course, once they had gone through some basics of rhetoric together, and Nikias had practiced and proven himself as much of a natural at it as Kallion had thought he would be, Kallion had to go with Nikias to Armoury Street to hear the results.

The Armoury Street wine shop was dark and crowded, the tables filthy, the customers loud, the wine itself abjectly awful. Kallion had been in worse places, but never of his own volition, and never to drink. He sat in a booth with Nikias and Nikias's friend Lysandros, a cup of what he could only assume was pickling brine in front of him, trying not to look nearly as ill at ease as he felt.

The radicals were a very mixed lot. Some of them looked like rich men's sons from the Marble Porches, with expensive haircuts and artfully sloppy mantles. Some looked like labourers and artisans. Quite a few of them were women. The ones Nikias seemed most friendly with—though to be honest, he was friendly with everyone—looked to Kallion like fellow freed slaves. Lysandros was the exception, and he didn't quite look like he belonged to either group; he was well-spoken and obviously not a labourer, but he lacked the expensive haircut of the Marble Porchers, and his mantle was not only untidy but actually rather grubby. He was friendly in an offhanded way, but he seemed somewhat preoccupied.

"You don't have to drink that," Nikias said, tapping the side of Kallion's cup and leaning close so that he could be heard over the noise. "I can barely drink it any more, since you introduced me to the good stuff—hey, that's something else you taught me. We'll go home and have something drinkable later."

"You are so good to me," said Kallion.

A woman came up to touch Nikias on the shoulder. "I heard a rumour you were going to speak tonight?"

Nikias grimaced. "Oh, are they talking about it? I guess I can't get out of it, then."

He was joking; when the time came for him to get up and speak, he didn't even hesitate. He rose and stood before his friends in the crowded, lamplit room. He looked relaxed, following all Kallion's instructions about how to stand and where to look to radiate confidence. Actually, Nikias deliberately radiating confidence was something of a daunting sight. He was glorious. Kallion felt an ache in his throat.

"Friends, I have not stood up to speak to you before. Maybe you are wondering why I would do it now." He pitched his voice just right—not hard, since it was a deep, resonant voice to begin with. "What do I have to say that could not be said better by Lysandros or one of our philosopher friends? I am not learned—I sign my name with an X—so why would you listen to my arguments? Well, I lived sixteen years in slavery, but many of you have lived more. Even if you have not been enslaved, you know what it looks like—it's not an unfamiliar thing for anyone in this city. Is it that I had an especially hard time of it? Well, no, actually—just the opposite. I was owned for sixteen years by a man I dearly loved."

He had practiced the speech at home for Kallion, but in front of the crowd at the wine shop he gave it with a controlled passion that he had not been able to summon before. Kallion listened spellbound. Nikias described his life in the mountains in simple terms, a brief sketch compared to the details he had told Kallion.

"All these were things that I thought and felt, but according to the law I was a thing. I might have starved to death if I had not been made into a thing by being sold. I only became a person again when my master died and left me my freedom in his will—or maybe he left me ownership of myself, the way he left the ownership of his other slaves to his wife? I don't know how it was written in his will. All I know is that I was the same, before and after, to myself. By the law that we have, as I've heard Lysandros say—and many of you have also said it in different ways in your speeches, so I hope I've got this right—I came back to life when I was freed. Because while I was in slavery, a thing, I might just as well have been dead. Well, I wasn't. I've been alive all along. That's why I know slavery to be wrong. It's founded on a lie."

There was applause, and Nikias's friends called out congratulations and approval. Nikias sat back down, flushed and obviously trying not to grin. He took a swig of the pickle brine and set his cup down with a bang.

"What did you think?" He looked at Kallion, eyes bright.

"It was splendid. You were splendid."

More than that, he was persuasive. He made Kallion want to join the radicals, against all his better judgement. Because Nikias was right; slavery was founded on a lie, a pretence that some people could be objects, as worthless as dead bodies, while they were still alive. It wasn't good enough to claw yourself out of that living death, or to help make it easier for a few others. The thing shouldn't exist at all.

"Give him a kiss," said Lysandros impatiently from the other side of the table.

That was when the door of the shop banged open, letting in a gust of cold night air, and someone burst in shouting something about the harbour.

"What?" a dozen people demanded.

"Shut the door, damn you!" another dozen yelled over them.

"—ships! In the harbour!"

"What?"

"Damn your eyes, the door!"

It took a minute for the message to get through to the back table where Kallion and Nikias were sitting, but finally it did.

*Grain ships. In the harbour. On fire.*

Kallion felt darkness gathering at the sides of his vision. Desperately he took hold of the cup in front of him and forced himself to swallow a mouthful of the terrible wine.

*Grain ships, two of them. On fire in the harbour.*

"Kallion?" Nikias was saying, peering at him with a worried look. "Are you all right?"

"Yes," Kallion managed. "I'm fine, just—it's not good news."

"I guess not," said Nikias. He looked across the table at Lysandros. "Is it … as bad as all that?"

"It's not good." Lysandros was also looking shaken. "All of Pheme depends on that grain. Your master, in the mountains, likely bought grain that had been imported on a ship from Gylph or Pyria for you to grind and make into his bread. The poor of the city queue up to get the grain dole every month, and that's where it comes from. The navy protects those ships fiercely. I don't know how pirates managed to get at them—and I don't know why they would. Just to burn them—it's suicidal."

"Do you suppose it was the Dodeki?" Nikias asked.

Kallion heard his voice as if from far away, and realized Nikias was speaking to him.

"I don't know," he said.

"Must have been." Lysandros shook his head. "Who else would have the resources to pull off a stunt like that? But it's insane. The navy will obliterate them."

Kallion took another swallow of wine. "Let us hope," he heard himself saying, but he wasn't sure he could any more.

# CHAPTER 19

THEY LOOKED out from Kallion's balcony when they got home, and saw the ships still burning, flames leaping from the rigging and the deck and flickering in reflection on the dark surface of the water.

"Do you think there was anyone on board when … " Nikias's voice trailed off.

"I don't know." Kallion's voice sounded flat. "The old Dodeki, in Photis's day, they would have got everyone off first. These days … " He shook himself. "Though it's worth remembering the crews on those grain ships aren't large— there are no oarsmen, to make more space for the cargo."

"Is Lysandros right, about what he said back there?"

"There may be shortages, if the government isn't able to arrange for more shipments—and if the Dodeki burn any more ships … It's true that we depend on grain from Gylph, and from Pyria and the colonies. But there is a substantial stockpile as well."

"I meant, was he right about what will happen to the Dodeki? The navy will wipe them out?"

"They will try to." Kallion stared fixedly at the flames out in the harbour. "It may not be as easy as your friend made it sound."

"Mm." Nikias leaned on the balcony rail. "It'd be good if it happens, though, right?"

"Good. Yes."

Something was obviously bothering Kallion, and he was obviously not going to say what. Nikias was used to this by now.

After a moment, without turning to look at Kallion, he said, "Why do you think they did it, then?"

When there was no answer, he turned to see that Kallion had already gone back inside the apartment. Nikias frowned, then followed him in.

They made love that night, but Kallion was strange, riding Nikias as if he was trying to hurt himself, and Nikias found himself talking less, offering less comfort than usual, because he didn't think it was wanted. Whether it was *needed*, though … well, he was tired, and they could always try to talk about it tomorrow.

In the morning, Kallion was up before him, packing his satchel in his study when Nikias emerged yawning from the bedroom.

"I'm going to be busy all day," Kallion said, glancing up briefly. "I have several important things—I'm afraid I'm not going to be free this evening."

"Oh." Nikias was nonplussed, but tried to keep it to himself. "Well, I do have a bed of my own—about time I used it again, eh? You haven't had breakfast yet, have you?"

"I have. Leftover pancakes from yesterday. There's plenty left for you."

"Right. Well, let me get dressed—you'll have to wait for me to eat, I'm afraid, so you can lock up after me."

It looked to Nikias as if Kallion hadn't thought of that, but he wouldn't go so far as to ask Nikias to eat his breakfast

in the street, so he paced around and sat stiffly on the opposite couch in the dining room while Nikias dressed and ate
breakfast. Nikias kept giving him quietly questioning looks,
offering Kallion the opportunity to explain himself and
becoming more and more annoyed when he never did. He
didn't exactly dawdle over his breakfast, but he certainly
didn't offer to take it with him to the market. They left the
house together, Kallion locked the door, and they walked in
silence to the corner where their paths diverged.

"Good luck with your work," Nikias said, relenting with
a smile. "Let me know when you're free. You know where to
find me."

"I do," said Kallion. "I will." He leaned in and gave
Nikias a kiss on the cheek, then turned away toward
Court Row.

Everyone in the market was talking about the grain ships, but
Nikias didn't hear the name of the Dodeki mentioned until
Itia arrived in the afternoon. He was surprised to see her
walking with a familiar figure, a man of about his own size
and colouring. They were holding hands.

"I told Tiko you might be able to give him some work,"
said Itia. "Sharpening the knives and cleaning—you were
saying it needed doing."

"Sure," said Nikias. "I can give you a half nummos for a
morning's work. Sound fair?"

"Sounds more than fair, sir."

"Don't call him sir," said Itia, poking Tiko in the ribs
with a finger. "He's just Nikias."

"Yeah, but he's the boss now," Tiko teased her. "You
mean to tell me you don't call him sir?"

"You know I don't. Get to work."

"So the two of you … ?" Nikias said, catching Itia's eye when Tiko's back was turned.

"Oh!" She waved a hand. "It's not—it's just. You know. "

"I had my eye on her ever since Master Epaphras took over the Shipyard Road house, is what it is," Tiko put in.

Itia rolled her eyes. "Me and everyone else in the household—and I mean *everyone*. But it's turned out we like each other. Don't we?"

"We do," said Tiko, grinning.

"I'm happy for you," said Nikias sincerely.

"Did you hear about the grain ships?" Tiko asked later, as he was sharpening knives. "Itia thinks it was the Dodeki, those pirates who worked for her old master."

"It had to be," said Itia, wielding a knife to begin chopping octopus.

"Kallion thinks so too," said Nikias.

"Kallion?" Tiko repeated. He looked at Itia. "Does he mean the Kallion from your old house?"

"They're a couple," said Itia. "Him and Nikias."

"Oh." Tiko gave Nikias a slightly wide-eyed look. "Since when?"

"For about a month now."

"Oh! That's great. He's a great guy! I like him a lot. Yeah, so, the pirates, huh? What do you think they did it for?"

"They'll probably demand ransom money," said Itia calmly. "You know, 'Pay up so no more unfortunate accidents happen to your grain ships.'"

"A protection racket," Nikias supplied, pleased that he remembered the term. "With the whole of Pheme as the victim."

Tiko whistled. "Gods. That's low."

"They're *pirates*, sweetheart," said Itia dryly.

Tiko looked at her, not laughing, and then he went and put an arm around her shoulders. "Never going back," he said, his voice low. "Never setting foot in that house again. All right?"

Itia leaned into him. "I know."

Tiko did a good morning's work and left with his half nummos. The lunch rush subsided, and Itia and Nikias were able to take a break in the afternoon. They sat on their stools behind the front counter, drinking cups of the tart, herbal vinegar-water that was being sold by the stall next to theirs.

"Are you hoping I'll be able to give Tiko more work?" Nikias asked, thinking it best to broach the subject directly.

"No, well—I know things are—"

"Because I might be able to. Oranteia just got engaged again, Pyke told me yesterday, and her fiancé is some kind of merchant—she's not going to need a job. So I'll be on the lookout for a new assistant, if you thought Tiko would want it. And if you want him around all the time—I mean, maybe you don't. Just because he's good company in one situation ... "

Itia laughed slightly. "He's a good man. And he does need work. If he had a job, he could ... we could ... maybe, I don't know. Anyway, it would help."

"Right," said Nikias, getting the gist. "He seems to care for you. I guess he knows what you went through in your old master's time."

"Yes. He knew, a little bit, even when he was in Master Epaphras's house, and we have talked." She sipped her drink. "You saw it when it wasn't so bad, Nikias. That night at the Euthalion? That wasn't so bad. That was after the master had been dead for six months."

"Kallion told me he was a hard man to serve."

"He was cruel," Itia said quietly. "I am glad he's dead—I think I've never been more glad about anything."

Her vehemence startled him. He'd never heard her talk like this before; maybe it had taken not just the death of

Hesteus but also her release from slavery in his house to make her feel she could speak the truth.

"What did he do?" Nikias found himself asking, even as he thought that he shouldn't, that she didn't want to talk about it, and he probably didn't want to hear.

"It wasn't so much *what* he did—it was how much he *liked* it." She shivered slightly. "He beat people for no reason, hanged people for no reason. You always feared what he would do when he *did* have a reason, but sometimes it was nothing. He would do nothing. Or he would wait weeks, months, until everyone else had forgotten what happened, and then he'd drag the person out into the garden and hang them, and make everyone watch—everyone always had to watch. He had a scaffold in the garden, just standing there, all the time. You can still see the holes in the ground for the posts. Sometimes he'd have us take the noose down for parties. Sometimes he wouldn't. It depended who was invited.

"He was cold as a stone, though. Not lustful—he never touched you except to hurt you. And he didn't like friendships among his slaves. That was one of the things he'd have us beaten for, if he saw us being friendly with one another."

Nikias remembered the camaraderie of his old household in the mountains, the friendly way his fellow slaves teased him about being the master's favourite. He felt sick.

"It's too horrible. Itia! How did any of you survive?"

She shook her head. "I don't think many of us did, really. I was only in the household a few years—I was lucky."

Kallion had been born there.

Itia looked up at him, sidelong. "I know who you're thinking about. I'm glad you're with him. He was ... He deserves something good."

She was silent for a long time, cradling her cup without drinking. Finally she said, "He always tried to make things better, in little ways. There wasn't *very* much he could do, or anyone could do. Just little things—making sure you got extra food and rest after a beating. Keeping an eye on people. You couldn't have friends in that house, it wasn't safe, but you could look out for people, and he did that.

"He's clever, too. He'd manage to make it look like he was following the master's orders exactly, even when he was letting little things slide. But people were scared of him. I'm sorry to say it. Just because he had some power—it wasn't very much at all. He was always careful not to see things that he'd be expected to report to the master, because—you couldn't ask anybody to just *trust* you, in a house like that. After the master died and Kallion was freed and left the house, we could all talk more, and we realized how much he'd done for us. I was sorry we hadn't all appreciated him more.

"So. I'm glad he has you to appreciate him now." She looked up at Nikias with a sad smile. "I don't suppose he's told you much of that himself?"

"Not much, no."

Nikias turned away for a moment to build up the fire under the fritter pan. He felt a deep ache inside, a sorrow and a tenderness that he didn't know what to do with. If Kallion were there, he would have hugged him so tightly. He would have said, "Don't you dare say you're not good enough for me ever again."

Kallion didn't come to the market stall that day, but that didn't really surprise Nikias. The impression he'd gotten that morning had been that Kallion wouldn't be coming. So he went back to his own room, which seemed at the same time cramped and echoingly empty.

The following morning he arrived at the market in a dirty tunic, with his hair looking fuzzy, because his clean tunic and his hair oil were both at his lover's house. He planned to joke with Kallion about it later in the day.

Satteia arrived just before the lunch rush, and approved

of Nikias's proposal to hire Tiko. She perched on a stool at the counter and munched a skewer of octopus fritters.

"This has been such fun, Nikias," she said, looking around the stall with satisfaction. "I hope you're having fun too?"

"Oh, absolutely."

She grinned. "I'm so glad Kallion talked me into becoming your patron."

"He—he did?"

"What, didn't you know that? Oh, it was entirely his idea. I told him I wanted to invest in some business, and he immediately suggested yours. I wasn't even thinking of a food business at all, and he had to convince me. Was the Tetrina Market your idea or his?"

"I, er—his, I guess." He didn't say that he had thought it was Satteia's. In fact, hadn't Kallion explicitly said it was Satteia's?

It was like the things Itia had told him. Kallion had gone about to do something to help Nikias, but he had done it secretly, sneakily, making it seem as if he'd had almost nothing to do with it. Maybe it was a habit with him now.

Kallion did not come to the market that day, either. Nikias closed up late, because the market had been busy. Another grain ship had drifted into the harbour in flames, and now the name of the Dodeki was on many people's lips. Something had happened to confirm that the pirates were responsible—Nikias heard someone suggest that the archons had received a ransom demand.

He thought about going to Kallion's apartment, remembering how Tiko had put his arm around Itia to comfort her the day before. He should be there to offer the same sort of comfort to Kallion, who was obviously in distress over the attacks on the grain supply, for reasons that Nikias didn't quite understand.

Unfortunately, he had promised to bring a couple of

Pyke's pans back to her after closing, as she was preparing to cook the food for her niece's wedding. By the time he had finished this, it was dark, and he was tired, and though he did walk back up the Tetrina Hill to Kallion's building, by the time he got there all the windows were dark. He trudged back down to the Vallina and slept in his own bed again.

# CHAPTER 20

THE FOLLOWING DAY, a fourth grain ship was set on fire. This time it happened in the early hours of the morning, and Nikias heard about it from his neighbours as he left his room.

It felt personal, somehow, to hear that there had been another ship burned. Nikias walked to the market brooding about it. Everyone was sure it was the Dodeki who were doing it, the same assholes who had crashed the Euthalion party at the Shipyard Road house, whipped Nikias, and done who knew what harm to Kallion and the rest of the household in the past. Now they were holding the whole city hostage, threatening the Republic with hunger for no good reason—just because they could.

Worry was thick in the air at the market. Everyone was jumpy and impatient, speculating and fretting. There was a rumour going around that something was wrong with Pheme's stockpiled grain, too, and that shortages were inevitable A fight broke out at a neighbouring stall when they ran out of hazelnuts. ("So stupid," Itia muttered, pounding a lump of dough with unnecessary violence. "It wasn't a hazelnut ship that caught fire.") In the afternoon, a wild-eyed man climbed up on the edge of the fountain and began making a rambling speech about how the pirates were in the pay of the archons.

It seemed such obvious nonsense to Nikias that he didn't expect anyone to pay attention to it, but a crowd began to gather. Customers emptied out of the seats around the lunch stall, as people either drifted toward the speaker or hurried away from him. Pyke arrived to report that her niece would not be able to come in that afternoon, and Nikias gestured to the empty tables and said it didn't matter.

Someone began heckling the speaker, then someone began heckling the heckler, and then a third party punched one of the hecklers-of-the-heckler. Then—and Nikias thought this was probably an accident, but it was hard to say for sure—someone knocked over a handcart full of fruit on the other side of the fountain.

After that, it escalated quickly to mayhem. The nut-seller's stall was ransacked, and that was definitely not an accident. People began throwing figs and persimmons and pushing each other into the fountain. The first thing Nikias did was to grab the pot of hot oil from the stove at the back of his stall and set it on the ground, pushed under the counter. Itia was busy putting out the cooking fires. There was a crash from behind them as someone threw someone else into the front counter and it splintered, raining fritters and pastries and sauce from sliding crockery. Nikias vaulted over the remains of the counter to help the man who had crashed into it, while Itia and Pyke together scrabbled for the salvageable dishes.

A child and a ragged man were already snatching up fist-fuls of the spilled food. Nikias accidentally trod on somebody's hand. The person yelped and drove their head into Nikias's groin, and he staggered back against the corner of the broken stall with an oath. The menu board clattered on the cobbles. Out of the corner of his eye, Nikias saw Pyke struggling with a woman trying to steal one of the frying pans. Another woman had opened the door at the side of the stall and was dragging out the crock of flour. Several stools had already been commandeered as weapons.

Pushing away the beggars crowding around the front of the stall, Nikias heaved himself back over the counter, where Itia had already grabbed the cash box. He slung an arm around her waist and caught Pyke with the other hand.

"Come on," he said. "Let's get out of here."

Pyke gave up without a fight, letting go of the frying pan and allowing herself to be hustled out the door with Itia, past the woman stealing the flour. Nikias forged a path through the crowd for the three of them, weaving and side-stepping the worst of the chaos, using his size and his shoulders where he had to, and they made it safely out of the square and into a quiet street.

"Nikias," said Itia, and he only then noticed that she was in tears. "Your beautiful stall!"

"The fuckers," Pyke snarled.

"It's just a broken counter and a few stools," Nikias said stoutly.

"It won't be, by the time they're done out there," said Pyke. "I'm going straight home and barring my door, and you two should too. I've seen riots in this city before—I remember the grain shortages in Agathon's time—and this will get a lot worse before it gets any better."

Nikias looked over her shoulder at the crowd in the marketplace. It had grown uglier in the few moments they had been standing here. He thought about alternate routes to get home.

"I'll walk you back to your house," he said firmly. "Itia, where are you staying?"

The market was in ruins: stalls flattened, goods strewn and squashed on the cobbles. The violence had abated by the time Kallion got there, after sundown, but the marketplace was not quite deserted. Small bands of looters picked over the remains of the stalls, and knots of people stood talking and arguing in doorways. Unease hung over the place like a low cloud.

It was difficult to find Nikias's stall, or what was left of it, in the dark and without the usual landmarks. The front counter had been destroyed, the interior picked clean by looters. The menu board that Kallion had written lay broken on the ground, and the banner that said NIKIAS'S had been half torn off the awning. Of course there was no sign of Nikias himself. No sign of Itia or the other assistant, either.

Kallion pulled his mantle tighter against the cold night air. He didn't know what he had expected to find, but he didn't know where else to look, either. A boy had come running into the clerks' hall hours earlier with the news that there was rioting in the Tetrina Market. Kallion had left his work and come up here, worried about Nikias, but he hadn't been able to get close to the place. By that time the riot was spreading into the neighbouring streets. People were marching with torches, shopkeepers were closing their shutters pre-emptively, and Kallion had turned back in the direction of Nikias's apartment, hoping to find him already there.

He wasn't. Kallion had sat on the gallery outside Nikias's door for a couple of hours, until he heard a report that the disturbance had died down. He wondered now what else he should have done.

*You should have been there*, a voice in his head suggested. *You shouldn't have pushed him away these last few days. You should have had the courage to tell him the truth.*

Nikias would have had the sense to get out of the area when the riot started, and it was unlikely that he would have been hurt. Devastated at the destruction of his stall, yes—

and Kallion should have been there to comfort him over that, or at least to try to.

He wouldn't be alone, wherever he was. He might be in a tavern somewhere, drinking with friends—fellow tradesmen from the market, perhaps—talking over the events of the day. He could have been in Armoury Street, but he probably wasn't; Kallion thought the radicals would have more sense than to gather on a night of unrest in the city. Nikias might be at Pyke's, and Kallion didn't know where that was.

He might be at Satteia's—if Satteia and her husband hadn't already left the city. Kallion could go to her house. But there was one other place he should check, just on the off-chance. He walked up the Tetrina Hill toward his own apartment house.

Nikias was sitting on the steps at the back, arms folded on his knees, staring at the paving stones. He didn't look up when Kallion approached, and so Kallion dropped down to sit on the step beside him, his body flooded with relief.

Nikias started. "It's you! I was beginning to be … "

"Me too," said Kallion. He put a hand on Nikias's knee. "I was looking for you in the market. I saw what happened to your stall. I'm so sorry."

"Wrecked, is it?" said Nikias. "I haven't been back to look. I took Pyke and Itia home, and then I went to Court Row looking for you."

"And I've spent the afternoon looking for you, in all the places where you weren't. The stall is a wreck—but if you and Pyke and Itia got away safely … "

"We did. I know, that's the most important thing." He squeezed Kallion's shoulder, kept his hand there, a warm weight. "Kallion, these past few days—what's the matter? Can you tell me?"

Gods, he should have known that Nikias would ask, and so gently, too. Kallion scrubbed his hands over his face.

"I've been afraid, Niki. Terrified. I still am. I've been

avoiding you because … because I didn't want you to know. Nikias, my old master isn't dead."

It shouldn't have felt like such a shock. Nikias had heard plenty of times that Hesteus was only *presumed* dead.

"How do you know?" he asked finally.

"The burning of the grain ships. It was a plan he had. He was going to get the Dodeki to attack the city's grain supply and then come to the rescue with another fleet of ships he was having built."

"Couldn't they just be doing it without him, because he gave them the idea?"

Kallion shook his head. "The other fleet, I know where it was, and it's gone missing. It can only be because he took delivery."

"So this was his plan. To hold the city hostage? Cause riots and starvation?"

"It's partly why I decided he had to die."

"You … "

In the dark, Nikias could just make out Kallion's profile, his dark hair falling around his face. Nikias had a sudden, lurching feeling that the man beside him was a stranger.

The slave who killed his own master was a special kind of monster. That was what everyone said. The crime was so terrible that in the days of the kings of Pheme, they used to execute the murdered master's entire household along with the slave who'd done the actual deed. They still did it, in some places. Nikias knew that because he'd heard his own master talk about it approvingly.

"I hired some of his own thugs to kill him," Kallion said, very calmly. "I knew them, you see, because I often had to pay them for other jobs. It was not difficult to arrange. I sent them a message that was supposed to come from one of my master's rivals, offering them money to betray him. I could pretend I did it mostly for the Republic, or for the other slaves in his household, and I was thinking of those things—but I did it mostly for myself."

After a long silence in which Nikias could not think of anything to say, Kallion continued, still in that same calm voice: "I told you Hesteus kept saying I could be useful to him when I became a lawyer—and he knew that he'd have to free me for that. I don't know if he ever really intended to do it, but he had me draw up a letter of manumission, around the time I turned twenty, and he kept it in his desk and used to show it to me sometimes. He didn't need to do that to make me do as I was told. I had seen my predecessor hanged in the garden for attempting escape. I had seen a lot of people hanged in the garden for much less than that. I think he showed me that letter for his own amusement.

"He made me ruin people, terrorize people—he made me drive people to do desperate things, to kill themselves, to kill other people. I tried to subvert him when I could, but it was all small stuff—giving someone more time to pay 'by accident' or pretending letters had gone missing when really I'd burned them. I told you how I tried to help Agron Phariades, by ruining him.

"I kept thinking maybe I could have done more if I'd had the courage to risk my life—but if I'd been found out and killed, someone else would have had to take my place—I don't know whether I lacked courage or if it just didn't make sense. So I did something else. I had him—tried to have him killed. I wish I could have done it myself, but he never gave me *those* skills.

"After he was dead—after I thought he was dead—I went to his desk and made sure the letter of manumission was sitting out where Epaphras could find it. I added a codicil with a gift of money for myself, 'In recognition of his loyal service.' It wasn't even a forgery—I had written the fucking letter myself. I took more money—a much larger sum—directly from his coffers and altered his ledger to make it appear it had been paid out to the Dodeki to repair a ship.

"I used some of the money to pay the killers, but I kept most of it. You must have wondered how I can afford this apartment and the running water and my wine collection and everything on a clerk's wages."

Nikias had wondered, in fact, but not very hard. He still said nothing. His heart felt overfull. This was what Kallion had been carrying all along. Of course he had not been able to tell Nikias this. Nikias had thought Kallion's secrets were small and personal, and he had imagined himself being able to laugh and offer comfort when he learned them, to reassure Kallion that of course it didn't matter, whatever it was. This was different. He couldn't deny that his first reaction had been gut-clenching horror.

"The only thing I've felt guilty for," Kallion said, his voice still steady and flat, "is taking all that money and my freedom without doing more for the rest of the household. At the time, I thought I was doing enough for them by getting rid of Hesteus. I don't know if I'd even have thought of trying to free myself if that letter hadn't already existed. It didn't seem to me that the problem was slavery, just that particular master. You're the one who opened my eyes—you made me see that all his other slaves deserved their freedom too. And you helped them get it. But you see why I can't be a radical. I'm a one-man slave revolt. You don't want me anywhere near your movement."

Nikias drew in a breath. "The only reason we don't want a slave revolt is because they always end badly. Is this going to end badly for you? If he isn't dead, is he going to find out you hired those men to kill him?"

Kallion shook his head. "I was quite careful—setting up layers of misdirection and so on."

"Right. So we don't have to worry about that?"

Kallion gave a bitter laugh. "We have to worry about the fact that I did not rid the world of this man—not only that, but he has come back stronger, he has come back to do the thing he was always planning to do. He's going into politics."

"He's whatting into *what*? He can't possibly—we're a democracy, and he's not even human. He had a scaffold in his garden!"

"He is going to save the Republic from the Dodeki and become a hero."

"The Dodeki work for him, though."

"Yes, they work for him, and he's told them to burn grain ships, and he's going to sail to the rescue with his private fleet and defeat them. I know he's going to do this because he *told* me. I wrote letters to the shipyards about building his new ships. He's been setting this up for years. Ever since he realized he was losing control of the Dodeki—destroying them will be a perk, as far as he's concerned, not a sacrifice."

"Shit. Does Epaphras know any of this?"

"Not the part about me trying to kill his brother, no. But I told him my suspicions after the first two grain ships were burned. He wanted to believe it was a coincidence—it wasn't until the Dodeki claimed responsibility that he was convinced. He and Satteia are leaving the city."

"Are you going with them? It would probably be a good idea."

Kallion shook his head. "Epaphras said the same thing, a little more forcefully. I can't. I bear too much responsibility." He rubbed his forehead with the tips of his fingers. "Nikias, I … I know I don't have the right to ask you to stay with me, now that you know this."

Nikias remembered something suddenly. "Is this what you meant that time when you said you weren't good enough for me, and some day I'd find out? I mean—this is what you meant, right? There isn't anything else?"

"There are lots of reasons why I'm not good enough for

you, Niki. But I think this is the worst thing I've done, yes, and it is what I was thinking of when I said that." He looked up at Nikias through his lashes for a moment. "I'm sorry. I concealed all this from you when you have been so honest with me."

"I … I don't want you to take this the wrong way, but I've been able to tell, for a long time, that you were … badly hurt, maybe almost broken, deep down. I knew there were things you weren't telling me. If I'd been going to get angry about that, it would have happened a long time ago." He huffed out a laugh. "Actually, I'm damned impressed. Hiring thugs to murder your master and then embezzling enough money to live in style and collect fine wines—that's the stuff of legends."

# CHAPTER 21

"WHAT DO WE NEED TO DO?" Nikias asked, just as if this was a problem that both of them were facing together. Maybe, by some miracle, it was. "Is he going to have any claim to you and the rest of his household, when he comes back? Legally, I mean."

"Legally, no—probably not, now that they've been freed. Epaphras may be liable for everyone's market price, though, which will ruin him. And returning us to his house is … only one of the things Hesteus could try to do to us."

"Yeah," said Nikias grimly. "I was thinking that too. So we should probably get you out of Pheme."

Kallion shook his head. "I can't leave. I'll show you why. Come—come up?"

"Of course."

Nikias put his hand on Kallion's shoulder and squeezed, and Kallion felt as if he would melt. How was it possible that it had not all ended when he'd told Nikias the truth?

He got to his feet, and Nikias followed him up the stairs and into the apartment. Kallion lit a lamp and walked into his study, the light revealing the pile of scrolls and tablets on his desk.

"You've, uh, been working hard," Nikias remarked. Normally Kallion's desk was much neater than this.

"I've been preparing a case." Kallion hung the lamp on a stand and reached for one of the tablets. He flipped it open. "This is a list of some of my former master's debtors, the ones who had failed to pay, along with the dates when they were punished. That is, the dates when their shops were burned down or their wives were abducted. It doesn't say that here, but I can tell you, in each case, what it was. I was responsible for relaying the orders and reporting back about their success.

"Here's another—this is a record of repairs made to the Dodeki's ships, including the names of their captains. These ones are letters from debtors begging for more time to pay. I used to have to write replies to those. These are all to do with the building of the fleet at Oxos, the ships that he'll use to defeat the Dodeki—there are dates that show how long he was planning this.

"You had all of this?" Nikias stared at the pile on the desk. "All these records?"

"They were in his house, mostly locked in a cabinet that I didn't have the key to. The house is empty now—I went back and broke into the cabinet, and I've been taking all this out and sorting it for the last few days. That's what I've been busy doing. Well, one of the things. I've got a couple of other irons in the fire that I can tell you about later, but this is the main weapon I have against him."

"Does Epaphras know?"

Kallion shook his head. "He has the key, and has seen some of this himself, though I don't think he has gone through it in detail—I don't think he had the stomach to. I asked if he would let me see it when I told him my suspicions, but he said no. So I broke in."

"What are you going to do with all this?"

Kallion chewed his lip, reluctant to say it aloud. Nikias

would try to talk him out of it. "Make a case before the Citizens' Assembly, when Hesteus comes back to Pheme."

"Yeah," said Nikias unhappily. "That's what I figured."

"I have to do something. I tried to get rid of him altogether, and it didn't work, and I … " He sighed and rubbed his forehead with both hands. "I can't do that again. I'm too afraid of what I might become, if I did something like that again. Even if it would just mean finishing a job that I started, I … "

"Yeah. It's like you're being given a second chance, or something?" Nikias still sounded unutterably glum. "I get it."

"Besides, I was a slave when I acted before—I couldn't have gone to the Assembly or testified in court or taken any legal action against him. Now I'm a free man, so I can."

"So you have to. Yeah," he said again. "I get it." He looked up at Kallion. "I'll stand by you, whatever you do. This doesn't change anything between us, Kallion—you know that, right?"

"I think I'm beginning to believe it," Kallion said softly.

"Can I take you to bed?" Nikias asked.

The bedroom was too cold for nakedness, so when they had shed their clothes they got quickly under the covers on Kallion's bed. They twined together, Nikias's hands sliding down Kallion's back, Kallion's slender legs wrapping around Nikias's waist. They kissed, tongues and limbs engrossed, loosening and opening to each other. Nikias rolled Kallion onto his back but did not enter him, just rubbed into his warmth, moving gently over him, kissing and caressing. For a while neither of them spoke.

"All right, sweetheart?" Nikias asked finally, looking down into Kallion's eyes. He stroked Kallion's soft hair back from his face.

"Ah, Niki." Kallion gave a breathy laugh. "I don't deserve this. To love you like this."

Nikias went still. "I think," he said finally, "if you want to, you do. I'm an all right person to love. I'll love you right back."

"You will?"

"I mean I do. I have for a long time now, I think. I just didn't think you'd necessarily want to hear about it. But now that we're being all honest with each other … " He shrugged, and Kallion laughed. "All right, you need a bit of attention here, don't you, my honey?"

He engulfed Kallion's smooth, hot dick in his hand and gave it a couple of practiced strokes. His own was so close, in the warmth under the blankets, that he touched them both at the same time. That sent a surge of heat through him. He'd never touched himself with someone else watching. He shifted back a little, letting the blanket fall away, so that he could use both hands, and rubbed, finding a rhythm that pleased him. It was so simple, nothing fancy, but so *equal*. Kallion had pushed up onto his elbows to look down at them, sleepy-eyed with pleasure.

"You want to, uh, feel me some other way, honey?" Nikias managed to ask. He slowed his hands, stroking again instead of rubbing, but he didn't want to let go.

"You're doing great," Kallion purred. "You keep going just like you're doing. I want to see how much you love it."

Nikias made a strangled sound; his chest heaved. He understood now why Kallion loved to be talked to like that.

"I'll—I'll try," he panted. "Thanks."

Should it have felt different? Nikias wondered, lying on his side with Kallion asleep in his arms some time later. He shifted his hips to ease himself out of Kallion's body. He'd taken Kallion in all the ways he liked. Should it have felt different now that he knew what the secret was that Kallion had been keeping? Maybe lovemaking wasn't the place where it would feel different. That was about bodies, after all, and their bodies had always been, if you could put it like that, honest with one another.

He nestled Kallion protectively against his chest. Hard times might be coming—they almost certainly were—but Nikias felt as if the two of them had passed through one trial together already. Like climbing up to a pass in the mountains, or something. There might be a long road ahead, and there might be bandits—pirates, whatever—but they'd made it up to that pass, and it was downhill from here.

# CHAPTER 22

KALLION WAS IN THE KITCHEN, mixing batter for pancakes, and Nikias had just stepped out onto the balcony when Kallion heard him exclaim, "Immortal gods! It's happening!"

They had a spectacular view; to see any more clearly, you would have had to be down at the harbour itself. The ships had sailed right into the mouth of the Phira: three of the Dodeki's galleys chasing a heavily laden grain ship. Or what *looked* like a grain ship, but when the sailors jettisoned their cargo and threw lines to a couple of barges that began towing it away up the river, it became obvious that this had been a trap for the pirates. When Kallion came out onto the balcony, pancake batter abandoned, four new galleys, bristling with oars, had emerged from around the shoulder of the bay and were bearing down on the Dodeki vessels.

"They outnumber the Dodeki," said Nikias.

"Not necessarily. It depends how many men are on each ship. But the Dodeki are trapped in the mouth of the river— it doesn't look good for them."

"I don't know who to cheer for here."

"We can be glad it's ending without any more grain ships set fire," said Kallion. "That's about all."

They stayed and watched; it was impossible not to. The decoy grain ship had disappeared from view up the river, hidden by the buildings of the city below. The two pirate ships furthest out in the bay put oars in the water and began moving smartly west, away from the city. The third took longer to exit the river's mouth, and was still stuck there when the foremost ships were attacked by the oncoming fleet.

All of Hesteus's galleys, as Kallion remembered from his correspondence with the shipyard, were equipped with rams. One of them struck a glancing blow off the side of a pirate vessel. The pirates wasted no time in throwing grappling hooks into the attacker and swarming across. The second Dodeki ship was not so lucky; it was grappled and boarded by the crew of one of Hesteus's other ships. Two more bore down on the galley still stuck in the mouth of the river.

"How many ships did Hesteus have built?" Nikias asked.

"Five. And I think that decoy grain ship was one, so we've seen all of them."

"And how many ships do the Dodeki have?"

"Anywhere from five to eight, depending on whether they managed to refloat the Ligeia, and whether any of the others have been sunk in the last six months."

"So those ships on the horizon," Nikias said, pointing, "those are more likely to be Dodeki than Hesteus."

Kallion shaded his eyes against the sun to look. There were three more ships approaching: sleek, fast-moving galleys with fearsome rams.

"Yes," he said grimly. "More likely."

Men were diving off the ship that had been taken by the pirates; from this distance, Kallion could just make out the tiny dark shapes hitting the water. It must have been holed in the collision, and it was sinking. It went down quickly, oars askew in the locks, mast sliding under the surface of the bay. The pirates took to their own oars, but one of Hesteus's ships gave chase and rammed them, this time hitting them solidly amidships. The pirate vessel began to take on water. There was fighting going on aboard the other ships now, and the Dodeki vessels on the horizon were approaching quickly.

And then, astonishingly, onto the scene sailed a sleek, small vessel: a nobleman's skiff. It darted in among the pirates, blocking an attack here, distracting the crew's attention there, a display of fancy sailing and sheer bravery that left Kallion staring open-mouthed.

Nikias whistled. "I don't know anything about sailing, but that's got to take guts, hasn't it?"

"Uh-huh," said Kallion. "I don't know who that is."

"It's not Hesteus?"

"Personally? Immortal gods, no. If he's on any of those ships, I'd be shocked."

He wasn't even sure what the pilot of the skiff was hoping to accomplish, at first. The three other Dodeki galleys had sailed right into the harbour, and the one that had been stuck in the river's mouth had got out and rammed one of Hesteus's ships.

"He's going to get himself killed," Kallion fretted. "Whoever he is."

Below them, the city was in uproar. All the rooftops that could be reached held watchers, people calling down details of the battle to their friends in the streets below. From here Kallion couldn't see the docks or the riverfront, but he could imagine they were thronging with people. His neighbours were running about in the street below.

"Look!" Nikias cried, pointing. "What are those? More ships!"

Kallion looked. Sails, half a dozen of them, on the massive galleys of the Phemian navy, sailing into the harbour to trap the Dodeki. Kallion knew why it had taken them so long to arrive; but apparently Hesteus's bribery could only achieve so much.

"I think the skiff was buying time," Kallion said. "He knew the navy was on the way."

Nikias turned away from the balcony railing and puffed out his cheeks. "Did you finish making the pancake batter? Because I think I might go inside and cook. I'm not sure that I want to watch the rest of this."

Kallion squeezed Nikias's shoulder. "Go ahead. I'll let you know what happens."

So Nikias, sweetheart that he was, retreated to the kitchen and made pancakes while Kallion leaned on his balcony rail and watched the Phemian navy destroy his former master's hand-picked pirates. From this distance, it was hard to guess how many prisoners were taken, how many men cut down by the soldiers aboard the naval ships, how many more dove overboard and trusted their fate to the deep water of the bay. Two of the Dodeki's ships were sunk, a third set fire; the rest were towed out of the bay behind the Phemian ships, back to the naval yards at Naupaktos.

It all seemed unreal at such a distance, like a dream or a spectacle. Kallion couldn't smell the smoke from the burning ship or hear the sounds of swords clashing or men screaming. He had never witnessed a battle before, and now it was hard to convince himself that this one had been real.

Nikias had the pancakes ready in the dining room when Kallion went in.

"Is it over?" he asked.

Kallion nodded. "The Dodeki are finished. Even if that wasn't all their ships, they won't come back from this. Not that Hesteus wants them to."

"He was lucky," Nikias said, sitting down and drawing up his legs onto the couch. "If the navy hadn't come when they did, that might all have ended badly for him. Or do you think that was all part of his plan?"

Kallion took a bite of a pancake and considered that. "I think he was lucky," he said finally. "And maybe unlucky, too. I think he meant to take down the Dodeki single-handedly, and he didn't quite do that, did he?"

They made their way down to the agora after breakfast, forging through crowds of people who didn't know quite what was going on, just that *something* had happened.

"He'll try to come up Victory Way, if he can," Kallion had told Nikias. "That's where victorious generals enter the city, and he'll have planned to do it that way, never mind that it'll look hubristic now."

Sure enough, there was a kind of procession spilling out into the agora from Victory Way as Kallion and Nikias arrived. It was led, unsubtly, by a number of people waving garlands and shouting rhythmically. When Nikias could make out their words, he realized they were chanting, "Saviour of the Republic! Saviour of the Republic! Hesteus!"

"It's a ritual thing," Kallion explained. "You're not *really* supposed to have your own men do it for you, but I've seen tackier things go on here, to be honest."

Following the garland-wavers came the crews of the ships, looking battered and sweaty and proud. As well they might, Nikias thought. They'd fought well, as far as he'd been able to tell, while they were outnumbered and probably outclassed, too.

"I doubt they know what he was up to," Kallion said, looking at the sailors. "He planned to go to some lengths to hire honest men for this job."

The chant about the Saviour of the Republic might have been started by Hesteus's own men, but it was being picked up by bystanders and people who were following the procession eagerly. Nikias watched for any sign of someone who might be Hesteus himself. Finally he spotted a man in an immaculate mantle, strolling behind the sailors, a little apart from the crowd, followed by a couple more people with garlands. He looked ordinary: a shorter, broader-shouldered, more sun-browned version of Epaphras. He didn't look like a monster, but Nikias had been bracing himself for that.

He glanced at Kallion.

"It's him," Kallion breathed, his eyes fastened on the man.

Nikias laid an arm around Kallion's shoulders.

Hesteus's procession crossed the agora, heading for the steps of the White Temple, where a number of important-looking men were already gathered.

"The serving archons," Kallion said, pointing them out to Nikias. "Hippophanes, Meliton, and Orantios. The men behind them are gerontes—you know, men eligible to vote in the Gerontion, the—"

"I know what the Gerontion is, thanks. My former master wanted to overthrow it along with the Citizens' Assembly and the Archonate and probably some other things that I've forgotten."

"Right. Sorry."

Nikias studied the three archons. Orantios, the youngest of the three, looked like he had just been roused from his bed. His fashionable haircut was squashed on one side, and he was yawning. The other two were middle-aged and more presentable.

"Shouldn't the naval captains get a procession too?" Nikias asked.

"Certainly, and they will. The gracious thing to do would have been to wait until they arrived before doing all this." He gestured at Hesteus's train. "But he's never been interested in doing the gracious thing."

"That seems like an understatement," said Nikias.

The garland-wavers were nearly at the temple steps when

another group emerged from a smaller street on the east side of the agora. They were waving things too, though these things seemed mostly to be people's hats and greasy paper from take-out food. They were cheering and yelling in a much less coordinated way than Hesteus's supporters.

"Polydoros!" Nikias could just make out. "Hooray for Polydoros!"

He remembered that this name belonged to the blond ex-archon whom he had seen at the Hippodrome with his children. And there was the man himself, being carried on the shoulders of a couple of his supporters and looking tolerantly uncomfortable about it. Beside him, another man had been hoisted up, this one flashily dressed in foreign clothes, with long hair under a mariner's cap and a scar sealing shut one eye. He seemed to be enjoying the attention much more than the scandal-plagued ex-archon.

"Why are they—" Nikias started.

"It was his yacht," Kallion said before he could finish. "And *she's* his pilot. Blessed Orante."

"Uh … she?" Nikias looked around for the woman Kallion was referring to, and realized he meant the person in the mariner's cap whom he had taken for a man. "Who is she?"

"Pantheras," said Kallion. "She used to be one of the Dodeki captains. The only one who survived the purge after Master Photis's death. And she's working for Polydoros, of all people!"

"Let's get closer," said Nikias, taking Kallion's hand. "I want to be able to hear what the archons say."

They found their way to a vantage-point close to the White Temple steps. They watched as both processions converged and dissolved, Hesteus's sailors joining in the enthusiasm for the yacht's pilot and owner, and Polydoros's supporters congratulating the sailors. They arrived at the foot of the temple steps as a confused mob.

Polydoros and Pantheras were deposited on the steps amid cheers. Hesteus separated himself neatly from the crowd and walked up the steps toward the serving archons.

Hippophanes gave a short, very pompous speech about civilian valour, and Meliton gave an even shorter speech that, as far as Nikias could tell, said exactly the same thing, and presented Hesteus with a wreath, looking rather bored about the whole thing. Then Orantios said something to his fellow archons, gesturing down the steps at Polydoros and Pantheras. There was some disapproving head-shaking before Orantios strolled down the steps, shook Pantheras by the hand, and gave Polydoros a sort of awkward nod.

"Let's go," said Kallion, tugging Nikias's cloak. "I think we've seen enough—and so far, we haven't *been* seen, and I'd like to keep it that way."

# CHAPTER 23

THEY WALKED BACK up the Tetrina Hill and stopped at the market to inspect the damage to Nikias's stall in the light of day. The market looked terrible, but the mood of the people who were milling around and cleaning up the debris was overall fairly bright. Everyone was discussing the morning's events, and Kallion heard the name of Polydoros on more than one set of lips.

"But I haven't heard anyone say 'Hesteus,'" he said with satisfaction. "This hasn't been the unmitigated triumph he has to have been hoping for."

"Outshone by a disgraced archon and a lady pirate," said Nikias, shaking his head.

"Well, I wouldn't call it a victory for us yet, either."

"I know." Nikias squeezed his hand.

They stopped in front of the ruins of Nikias's stall. It looked a very little less bad than it had the night before. Someone had put back the menu board, righted the tables, and restored most of the stools.

"Nikias," said a man's voice, and Tiko from Epaphras's household emerged from the inside of the stall. He noticed

Kallion and offered a friendly nod. "Kallion. Morning. What a mess, eh?"

"Yeah," said Nikias. "Though there's more left than I expected."

"I figure we can rebuild. The mistress—I mean Satteia—asked me to take a look around, see what I think. She's over there." He nodded toward a figure wrapped in a red mantle, sitting on the edge of the fountain. "She's, uh. Taking it hard, I think. Actually, I'll be honest, I've no clue what's going on."

"I thought she was leaving the city with Master Epaphras," said Nikias, looking at Kallion.

"That's what I thought," Kallion said. He frowned. "Let's go talk to her."

Of course what he meant was, *You go talk to her, Nikias.* He had no idea what to say to Satteia, under the present circumstances; it had been hard enough telling Epaphras that his brother was probably alive.

She looked up as they approached the fountain. Her face looked drained, her eyes larger and darker than usual.

"Nikias," she said, standing. "You're all right. The gods be praised."

"I'm fine," said Nikias heartily, taking her hand and pressing it briefly. "Itia and Pyke and I got out safely, and we managed to save the cash box, but not much else. Though it looks as if more of the stuff than I expected was left behind by the looters."

"We will rebuild," said Satteia, so fiercely that Nikias swayed back a little. She sounded like someone swearing vengeance on her father's killer. Then she turned to Kallion. "You know Epaphras has fled to the countryside. But I couldn't go with him. I think you feel the same. We have to do something."

"I'm planning to speak in the Citizens' Assembly," said Kallion simply. "They will meet on Moon's Day and propose honours for Hesteus. I'll stand up and say what I know about him."

Satteia nodded. "My husband should be here doing the same. I would if I could. You'll tell me if there's anything you need?"

"Where are you staying?" Nikias asked. "Kallion, do you think it's safe for her to stay at her house? It isn't, is it?"

"Where are *you* staying?" she countered, looking at Kallion.

"We're going to Nikias's place."

"It doesn't have a kitchen with running water," Nikias joked stoutly, "but Big H doesn't know where it is. Hey, I know, Pyke could probably put you up—she's got a nice place in East Vernina, and since her niece has moved out again, they have a spare bedroom."

Satteia was looking at him with one eyebrow raised, and Kallion almost shushed Nikias. She was a fashionable, rich woman who had maintained her own household for a decade while living apart from her husband. She wasn't going to accept the offer of Pyke's niece's old bedroom.

"All right," she said, with a humorous twist to her lips. "It sounds like fun. And, as you say, 'Big H' wouldn't know where to find me."

The Citizens' Assembly was to meet two days later, on Moon's Day. The day between, the city seemed strangely quiet, no rejoicing or rioting in the streets. Nikias spent a lot of time walking around, running errands that he had come up with for himself, to give Kallion time to work. He fetched food from cookshops, visited Satteia at Pyke's house, and took a cake that Pyke's sister had baked to Itia and Tiko. He checked up on a couple of other friends, bringing food and sharing drinks where he could.

Nikias's tiny room was knee-deep in Hesteus's records and correspondence, which they had ferried over from Kallion's study the night before. Kallion had to leave the door to the gallery open in order to have enough light to work by. At night they snuggled close on the narrow bed. Nikias didn't really feel like making love with all those evil scrolls and tablets in the same room with them, but he didn't say so. Kallion had lived his whole life around things like this. He spread Kallion out as much as the space would allow, face down on the bed, pulled up the blanket, exposing him from the waist down, and teased him with oiled fingers until Kallion was writhing and rubbing himself against the mattress, then flipped him over and finished him off with his mouth.

It rained on the morning of Moon's Day, a light drizzle that seemed to hang in the air rather than falling. They walked to the Civil Palace together, Kallion carrying his satchel with a selection of documents that he planned to present to the assembly.

When Nikias asked some question about the layout of the building, as they were climbing the steps, Kallion reminded him, "I've never been in here before. Half a year ago, neither of us would have been allowed in."

That suddenly brought home to Nikias what a daring thing Kallion was about to do, and how much courage it was taking for him to do it.

"Well," Nikias said, looking critically around the porch of the Civil Palace, "I don't think much of it so far. Kind of … old."

Kallion laughed and squeezed Nikias's arm. "Thanks. You're really doing an excellent job keeping up morale."

He hadn't thought of it in those terms, but of course that was what he had been doing. It was the main contribution he could make.

They entered the Civil Palace, and even Nikias did have

to admit that it was an impressive place. He'd been joking when he said that it wasn't. The ceiling was incredibly high overhead, the walls patterned with columns and panels of different coloured marble and things like doorways with statues standing in them. The floor was a giant mosaic in shiny, multi-coloured stone. At the end of the hall was a statue twice the height of a man, of a woman with a shield in one hand and a helmet tipped back on her head.

"Anaxe?" Nikias guessed, leaning toward Kallion to whisper because the hall was already filling up with citizens.

"That's right," said Kallion, and smiled at him.

Though he had not known anything about the building itself, Nikias had heard something about how the assembly that met there functioned. Not because anyone had ever told him directly, but because he had listened sometimes when he was serving in his master's dining room.

The Civil Palace was the seat of Phemian democracy, the place where any citizen could stand up and speak or vote on the questions brought before them. Of course not all the questions were brought before them, only kind of a mixed bag of things that were traditionally decided by the people rather than by the archons or the Gerontion. Nikias's master and his friends had always been a bit torn about this, and it had been a popular topic of discussion at dinner. They liked tradition, but they distrusted the common people and didn't like the idea of them deciding issues. Nikias had never in those days thought of himself as belonging, even potentially, to the "common people," so he hadn't had an opinion.

Now he did, decidedly. When he stood in the hall of the Civil Palace, he felt proud to be a part of the Republic. He was proud to be able to stand here with his fellow citizens, the ones in dusty labourers' tunics and the ones in gold-bordered mantles, and know that he had a role to play, small as it might be, in the democracy that governed the island.

After that, it was a let-down that the meeting of the assembly was incredibly boring.

Nikias had somehow vaguely expected, without really thinking about it, that the whole thing would be about Hesteus Photionis, and most of it would be taken up by Kallion giving a brilliant speech. It wasn't, at all. There was some business about repairing roads, somebody got up and gave a mumbled speech about traffic through the Portina Gate, somebody else gave a loud, ranty speech about foreigners, and the presiding archon—Orantios, looking even more like he'd just rolled out of bed than he had two days ago—cut him off, with an eye-roll that Nikias could see from where he and Kallion sat halfway down the hall.

He was just about to lean over to Kallion and ask when their business was likely to come up, when he saw that the next speaker walking to the dias was Tychon Taurides, whom he knew from Armoury Street.

"Citizens," said Tychon, reading from a tablet he had brought with him, "I come before you to speak of a smear of mud upon the honour of our Republic."

Someone laughed audibly, and Nikias couldn't entirely blame them. Tychon went on, still reading from his tablet. He didn't mumble like the first speaker—he was quite audible—but that was all you could say for him. It was a terrible speech. The smear of mud, of course, was slavery. He was giving a speech in support of abolition. No one was listening to him. A few people heckled, but most didn't bother, just chatted among themselves, ignoring Tychon.

They'd heard this before, of course. Nikias had heard Lysandros trying to recruit volunteers to speak in the assembly, but he hadn't realized what it meant. It meant getting up in front of this disinterested and hostile crowd, month after month, and trying to tell them something they didn't want to hear.

Nikias leaned toward Kallion and drew breath to speak.

"Yes," Kallion whispered.

"Yes what?"

"Yes, you could do a better job of that. I assume that's what you were going to say."

"Uh. Yeah. But it was going to sort of be a joke."

Kallion shook his head. "It's not a joke. You could do far better. I hope some day you will—if you want to."

They sat and listened to the rest of Tychon's speech, which didn't get any better.

"Thank you, Taurides," the bored archon said when it was over, rearranging his mantle. "Now, um … the assembly is asked to consider a nomination for the Gerontion." He gestured to a proclaimer at his side, who stepped forward.

"Hesteus Photionis," the proclaimer read out in a bellowing voice, "on account of extraordinary services rendered to the Republic on Seventh Day last, is thought fit to be elevated to the status required to serve on the Gerontion of the Republic of Pheme—so declares Phoronemos Melitiades."

A man briefly bobbed up from his seat to acknowledge that he was Phoronemos Melitiades. Kallion made a small noise of recognition, probably because he had written threatening notes to be delivered to the man in the past.

"Does anyone, um, want to speak to this?" the archon asked boredly. "Or … "

Kallion got to his feet.

# CHAPTER 24

"Hesteus Photionis is not a fit man to sit on the council which governs this republic," said Kallion. His voice carried through the hall, but with a much more pleasant cadence than the proclaimer's. He made you want to listen to him. "I speak to you as his former slave. You may well gasp— I know how shameful it is for a freedman to speak ill of his former master, much less in the Civil Assembly. I have no hope of winning your approval of myself. I only hope to spare the Republic suffering and ill governance at the hands of a man I know all too well to be brutal and without humanity.

"I know that there are others among you who can attest to the truth of what I say. I do not expect you to speak out— I speak out now so that you may keep yourselves safe by remaining silent. But we know how Hesteus Photionis made his money. We know that he had a network of 'clients' across the city, shopkeepers and artisans from whom he demanded regular, substantial payments in return for 'protection.' Protection from what? Protection from Hesteus Photionis, of course—or, more precisely, from the criminals he employed to smash and set fire to the homes and workshops of his clients. Some among you are shocked that I should make such a terrible allegation. Some among you know that I am speaking the truth.

"By itself, this scheme for extorting money from honest businesspeople provides only a portion of Hesteus Photionis's wealth. In most years, only about half. I was his secretary—I can speak to these numbers. I could show you a list of his 'clients,' too"—Kallion held up one of the scrolls he had brought with him to the dais—"were I not reluctant to reveal the names of the men and women whom he has ruined, lest they or their families suffer further for it. Besides the extortion, he had another source of income—the sale of slaves taken from the coasts of the Pseuchaian League and the neighbouring islands by the pirate crews of the Dodeki."

So far, Kallion's speech had been met with a mixture of muttering and shocked silence. Now the muttering grew louder, and there were a couple of outraged exclamations.

"I understand," said Kallion, spreading his hands. "I know. You think I must have got it wrong. Hesteus *destroyed* the Dodeki—well, he helped to destroy the Dodeki, he was certainly *trying* to destroy the Dodeki when he lured them into the harbour and attacked their ships with his own fleet. He might have done them some serious damage even if Polydoros and the Phemian navy had not come to his aid—he was clearly prepared to sacrifice his own ships to save the grain supply of the Republic. All this is admirable! Or it would be admirable, if he had not ordered the Dodeki to attack the grain ships in the first place."

This was when the hall finally erupted, and even now, it wasn't mayhem. There was something focussed about the outrage. Men were booing, but whether at Kallion or at Hesteus wasn't clear—Nikias thought it might have been some of each. People shouted things like, "For shame!" and "How dare he!"

Someone's voice cut across the others to declare, "He's

right!" But that person lapsed quickly back into silence, and no one seemed to be able to figure out who it had been.

Nikias remained silent, trying to look appropriately shocked so as not to draw attention to himself. He wished he had talked over with Kallion beforehand what kind of response would be helpful. Should he have been the one shouting, "He's right"?

Kallion held up a hand and made a motion as if patting the air. When the crowd quieted enough for him to pitch his voice over them, he spoke again:

"You are right to be outraged! My fellow citizens, you are right to disbelieve me—not because what I say is a lie, but because it is so outrageous. This hall is filled with honest men who cannot believe that anyone would be so base as to act in the way that I have described. You cannot believe that anyone could drive his freedman to speak out *truthfully* against him in the way that I have just done. It does you credit! I cannot expect you to believe me. I can only implore you—ask your neighbours, ask your colleagues and your friends, ask the shopkeepers in your neighbourhood. Let them tell you what they know of this man, and decide whether what I say could be true. Do not allow Hesteus Photionis to stand nominated for the Gerontion of the Republic until you know."

Kallion turned to descend the dais. The presiding archon beckoned him over and said something to him, then let him go.

"So … Anybody else want to speak to that?" the archon said, slouching in his chair, as Kallion left the dais.

There was dead silence for a few moments. The archon sat up and cleared his throat. Then the man who had made the nomination rose to his feet.

"That was all lies," he said, staring straight ahead. His voice shook slightly "Hesteus Photionis is an honourable man."

"A saviour of the Republic!" someone else called out helpfully.

"Yes. An honourable man and a saviour of the Republic."

"The slave is lying!"

"Freedman, you goat-fucker!"

"Civil language or you will be ejected," the proclaimer droned, obviously something he'd had to say many times.

Kallion arrived back at his seat beside Nikias and dropped into it. He looked exhausted.

"You were amazing," Nikias whispered. "What did the archon say to you?"

"Invited me to a party at his house."

"Not really?"

"Yes, really."

"I thought Hesteus Photionis was dead!" someone yelled.

"Yeah! How do we know it's really him?"

"So … " said the archon, "should we have a vote, or … not?"

"Request an adjournment, lord archon." The man who had made the nomination popped up again. "I request an adjournment. Before we vote."

The archon frowned and turned to his proclaimer to ask him something—maybe what an "adjournment" was. "Right. We'll adjourn until tomorrow. I think? Yes. Tomorrow. At the usual time."

He gestured to the proclaimer, who came smartly forward and shouted a formula to end the assembly.

"Let's get out of here," said Kallion, grabbing Nikias's arm.

"It was spectacular," said Nikias, for perhaps the tenth time, ladling out barley and sausages into bowls in Pyke's kitchen. "You should have heard him. Women should be allowed in there anyway, it's not fair that you're not, but you should have been today especially, because that was such a speech!"

Kallion buried his face in his hands, smiling down at the table.

"What happened? Did people believe him? Did they refuse the nomination?" Satteia asked eagerly.

"They, uh—what was the word? Adjourned. That means they're going to meet again tomorrow and vote then."

"Is that good?" Pyke asked doubtfully.

Kallion looked up. "It's good. It's what I was hoping for. I didn't think I could get them to vote the nomination down altogether, just on my word." He hadn't been altogether lying when he said he thought the Citizens' Assembly had more integrity than that. "But postponing it, hopefully, will give people time to start talking. Maybe some of his victims will decide to speak up."

"That crazy metal-worker who attacked you, remember?" said Nikias. He set a bowl in front of Kallion and distributed the others around the table, two bowls in each hand, making it look easy, as he always did. "Or the fellow from the clerks' hall with the grievance? Maybe they'll resurface."

"I've already sent messages to both of them," said Kallion.

Nikias, moving around the table behind Kallion's seat, paused to drop a kiss in Kallion's hair.

"You're a genius," he said, "and I—" He stopped, looking into Kallion's eyes, and he didn't need to finish the sentence.

"Me too," Kallion replied.

Satteia sat down at the kitchen table opposite Kallion. "You can say you love each other in front of us, you know," she said dryly. "We don't mind."

The kitchen door swept open to admit Itia and Tiko, arm in arm. Itia shook the raindrops off her cloak, and Tiko took off his hat and hung it up.

"Sorry we're late," Itia said. "We almost ran into someone in the street, and we had to wait until he'd gone."

"It was Skopo," said Tiko with obvious relish. "You know, the pirate?"

"I remember him," said Nikias, wincing. He had taken a seat next to Kallion, but he got up again to fill more bowls for the newcomers.

"He looked worse for wear," Tiko reported. "I dunno if he was on one of those ships that sank, or what, but he had a couple of his crew with him, and they looked spitting mad."

"What were they doing?" Satteia asked. "Just strolling about the city?"

"Looking for Master Hesteus," said Itia. "I heard them say so."

"I guess he's not at his house," said Nikias. "Because they certainly know where that is."

"I mean," said Satteia, "if I'd betrayed a bunch of pirates like that, I'd go into hiding. Actually, I am in hiding, aren't I?" She reached for a piece of bread from the dish Nikias had just set down. "But enjoying it," she said, smiling around at the table.

Kallion looked around at the room too: at Tiko and Itia, whispering something to each other and holding hands as they sat down at the table; at Pyke, bustling about her warm, cozy kitchen with her hair tied up in a kerchief, unwilling to let Nikias do all the work of feeding her guests; at Satteia, across the table from him, incongruous in her expensive red gown and her gold earrings; at Nikias, sitting down beside him again. Beautiful, generous Nikias, who had changed everything.

"What?" said Nikias, quirking an eyebrow at him.

"Nothing, I—I'm happy to be here. Thank you," he said formally, turning toward Pyke but including the rest of those present, "for inviting me."

There was an awkward pause. It had been an awkward

thing to say. They were all so easy with one another, and he wasn't sure that any of them except Nikias really liked him. They had no reason to; they had all known him as a creature of Master Hesteus, not to be trusted. But they had let him sit down to a meal with them; they were talking approvingly of what he had done at the Civil Palace that morning. They didn't even seem to mind that he loved Nikias.

"You're welcome any time," said Pyke gruffly. "Now, let's eat."

# CHAPTER 25

IT WAS VERY LATE when they walked back to Nikias's room, and considering that they had heard there were pirates wandering the streets, it was probably not a good idea for them to be out so late. They should probably have taken Pyke up on her offer of a bed for the night, but the 'bed' was going to have been a mattress on the kitchen floor, and Nikias had some specific ideas of things he wanted to do to Kallion that night that he couldn't see doing on Pyke's kitchen floor.

Of course, those things might have to wait anyway, because by the time they climbed the stairs at Nikias's building, Kallion was looking nearly asleep on his feet.

"You've had a long day, my honey," said Nikias, putting an arm around him. Kallion leaned into him, nuzzling his neck.

Nikias heard several sets of heavy footsteps on the stairs below them, unusual at this hour. He hurried Kallion on and reached the gallery on his floor.

His apartment was halfway down, and they had reached the door by the time the men following them arrived at the head of the stairs. Nikias got his key out and opened the door quickly, telling himself over and over: *Maybe it's nothing, maybe it's nothing.*

"Kallion," said a deep voice from down the gallery.

Kallion turned under Nikias's arm and went still. He said nothing. Finally Nikias made himself look down the gallery toward the stairs.

Hesteus was approaching at a stroll, a hand tucked casually into the front of his mantle. Two rangy, scarred men with cudgels followed him.

"It's nothing personal," Hesteus said, and Nikias realized the man was talking to him. "I'm afraid you have some property of mine there. I'm going to need you to return him."

"Don't even think about coming near him," Nikias growled, putting his body between Kallion and Hesteus. "You inhuman pig-fucking lizard of a bastard."

Lysandros would be proud of him, Nikias thought. That was some really interesting swearing. He felt light-headed with fury.

Hesteus gave a surprised laugh. "Excuse me? Kallion, if you want to keep your brute here alive, you'd better recall whose property you are."

Kallion stepped out from under Nikias's arm. "I do," he said. "No one's. You remember you had me write up an article of manumission. It must have occurred to you that your brother would enact it after you disappeared."

Hesteus narrowed his eyes. "He freed you."

If Nikias had to guess, he'd have said the man actually hadn't known this. He wondered suddenly what Hesteus had been doing since returning to Pheme. He hadn't been staying at his house—had he even been back there? Did he know about the freeing of the other slaves?

"You'll never really be free," said Hesteus calmly, inspecting the fingernails of his right hand. "After the things you've done?" He made a *tsk*ing sound that was the most sinister thing Nikias had ever heard. "No, I'm not letting you go. Slave, freedman, it doesn't matter. You're mine. And I've spent half a year in hell and plan to get my own back now I'm out. You must have wondered how I survived. Gorgion Pandares tried to have me murdered—suborned a couple of my own men to stab me in Lower Goulina. But they were greedy, the bastards. Greedy and stupid. They thought they would make some extra money selling me instead of killing me. Maybe they didn't realize how much of the slave trade in the Pseuchaian Sea flows through the hands of men who owe me favours. Maybe they thought I'd be grateful to them for sparing my life. They've already learned I don't take that view of the situation." Hesteus looked at Nikias. "Has he told you I was a hard man? Do you think a trip to Gylph on the oar of a slave-trader's galley will have improved my disposition?

"You're coming with me," he said to Kallion. "Now."

"No—" Nikias could see Kallion swallow the word *sir*. "No, I am not."

Hesteus laughed. He gestured to the men behind him. "Throw him over the edge," he said.

"No!" Nikias shouted, hurling himself between Kallion and the two men.

And then nothing happened. Of course nothing happened—he should have remembered. This was one of the "irons" Kallion had had in the fire. He'd gone around to all the likely men in town before Hesteus reappeared, offering to double whatever Hesteus paid them if they could get taken on as his guards. He had told Nikias all about it, but of course in the moment, Nikias had forgotten. He stood there, shielding Kallion from a threat that was not coming.

Hesteus looked around at his men. "Throw him over the edge," he repeated savagely. "Throw them both over the edge if you have to."

"Sorry, sir," said one of the men, sounding genuinely apologetic. "We're not working for you, is the thing."

"And we don't actually kill people," added the other, less apologetic. "We're bodyguards."

"He paid you to guard me?" Hesteus snarled incredulously.

"No, to guard him. I guess he was afraid you'd try something like, you know, this."

"You're doing a great job, though," said the other man, looking past Hesteus to give Nikias an encouraging smile.

"Hey," said Nikias, "if you were enslaved in Gylph, Hesteus, that makes you our equal, any way you look at it. Congratulations on your freedom, I guess? That's the traditional thing to say."

"Who the fuck is this?"

"This is Nikias." Kallion was grinning.

Hesteus stared glassily for a long moment, and when he spoke, his voice was a low growl. "It was you, wasn't it? Aristygion told me someone got up in the assembly today and blackened my name, saying I should never be elected to the Gerontion. Rumours are circulating, Aristygion said. People are talking. I thought you might know who it was. I'd have made you tell me. But it was you, wasn't it? You little shit. My father trained you up to be an orator, like you'd train a dog to fetch a stick, and you stood up in the Citizens' Assembly and betrayed me."

"Betrayed you? Did I owe you anything?"

"You hired these apes—what else did you do? *What else did you do?*"

"Um, sir? Not you, him." The bodyguard spoke over Hesteus's head to Kallion. "Do you want us to escort him home?"

"If you would be so good," said Kallion.

"I *will* have my revenge." Hesteus's voice shook with rage. He turned and stalked ahead of the bodyguards back toward the stairs. Kallion stood rigid, watching him go, and Nikias stood watching Kallion, waiting for the moment of collapse. It didn't come. Hesteus and the bodyguards disappeared down the stairs, and Kallion turned toward Nikias, head high, looking quite calm—even a little triumphant.

"My honey, I'm so proud of you," said Nikias, opening his arms.

Kallion walked into them and hugged him fiercely.

"We can't stay here," he said, stepping back. "He means it when he says he'll have his revenge. I've dealt him a blow, but we can't fool ourselves. He still has plenty of allies in Pheme —or at least people who are scared enough of him to do his bidding."

Nikias nodded. "What should we do?"

"Pack up as many of the documents as we can, tell the fire patrol to pay special attention to this building in case Hesteus sends someone back here, and then … find somewhere to sleep. Tomorrow I'll speak in the assembly again and then I'll—we'll—leave Pheme."

They ended up back at the ruin of Nikias's stall in the market. It was cold for sleeping outside, but they piled some empty sacks under one of the counters, crawled in together and curled up under their cloaks. Kallion lay with his head on Nikias's shoulder, and Nikias rubbed Kallion's back.

"You know the way I talk to you when we make love?" said Nikias thoughtfully. "You know that's not really how I feel about you, right?"

"No? What do you mean?"

"I mean, I like treating you like that in bed—like you … need encouragement. But really, I—well, I admire you. I'm in awe of you, sometimes. I was today."

Kallion got an arm around Nikias and hugged him tightly again, burying his face in Nikias's warm chest.

"You've made my life bearable to me, Niki, in a way that it wasn't before. I don't know what I was before I met you."

"You were wonderful then, and you're wonderful now. But I make you happy, I guess, and that's the best feeling in the world."

"If you don't want me to go back to the Civil Palace tomorrow … " Kallion began. "If you want to leave the city first thing in the morning, leave the island, even—I don't want you to be in danger because of me. 'Don't want' isn't strong enough. I'd rather die than have anything happen to you because I was too intent on destroying my old master. It's not worth that to me, not remotely."

"It's not just about that, though, is it? It's about keeping him out of the Gerontion. And Satteia's right—we've got to do that, we can't just slink off to the country like Epaphras."

"We may have accomplished that already," said Kallion. "I'm starting to think his nomination won't stand."

Nikias was tracing a pattern over Kallion's back with his index finger. "I'll miss the city," he said, around a yawn. "But if we have to leave, then we'll leave. Together."

"Together," Kallion murmured.

He fell asleep and didn't dream, waking disoriented and stiff in the dawn, to noises of the market sellers setting up for the day. Nikias was already up, trying to convince a woman on the other side of the counter that though he had a fire going on the stove and was frying something in a pan, the stall was not in fact open.

"Well, when will you open, then?"

"I'm afraid I can't say. Not until I've had a carpenter in to fix the counters, at any rate!"

"What, you mean you're closed *all day*?"

"All day, yeah. Probably for a few days … "

The woman made a *hmph*ing noise and flounced away. Nikias glanced over his shoulder.

"Good morning, beautiful. You hear that?"

"Yes," said Kallion, sitting up and raking back his hair. "It's lucky she didn't see me and ask whether you are running an inn here, and how much for a bed?"

Nikias guffawed. "I found a few eggs and a little jar of honey at the back of a shelf here that the looters apparently overlooked. I'm making an omelette for breakfast. You want some?"

"Yes, please!"

Kallion crawled out from under the counter, and they perched on stools inside the stall and feasted on fluffy egg straight from the pan, dripping with honey.

"Do you remember the first time you ate my cooking sitting in my stall like this?" Nikias asked, finished his half of the omelette and watching Kallion eat.

"Of course."

"Yeah, I guess it's not a happy memory for you. Sorry."

"It wasn't a good day, no," Kallion said slowly. "But you picking me up and dusting me off and feeding me octopus fritters—that is a good memory. It's a good reality."

Finished their breakfast, they walked to the public baths, then visited a barber, mundane things to occupy their time until the fourth hour, when the assembly reconvened. Kallion was hauling around his satchel stuffed to a comical size with scrolls and tablets from Hesteus's office. With nothing left to distract them, finally they walked down to the agora. It was crowded, with knots of people standing around talking. Kallion and Nikias ignored them and walked straight into the Civil Palace.

It was empty.

"I didn't think we were that early," said Nikias, looking around at the hall.

"We're not," said Kallion.

He looked back out the open doors at the people standing around in the agora, deep in conversation. Something had happened.

The proclaimer from yesterday came out of a side door toward them. "Hello! You're the gentleman who spoke yesterday. Magnificent job, I must say. And brave of you to stand up like that. Well, if you're here for the assembly today, of course it isn't happening. That was the last item of business, and the lord archon told everyone to go home. He wasn't particularly pleased about having to be here himself."

"Why has it been called off?" Kallion asked.

The proclaimer's eyebrows rose. "You can't nominate a dead man for the Gerontion, can you?"

"A *what*?" Nikias burst out.

"Oh, Hesteus Photionis is dead. Found dead in his house this morning, by his brother, I believe. Quite an unpleasant business, I'm told," the proclaimer added with relish.

They left the Civil Palace in stunned silence. Nikias reached for Kallion's hand on the steps outside.

"Do we—" he started.

"Have to go back to the Shipyard Road?" Kallion finished for him. "*I* do, certainly. I need to see his body before I believe it this time. You don't have to come, but I'd like it if you would."

"Don't be ridiculous. Of course I'm coming."

There was no huge doorman on duty at the Shipyard Road house today. The door was opened by a freedwoman whom Nikias recognized from Satteia's household.

"We're a house in mourning, we're not—" she started half-heartedly. "Oh, it's you. Better come in."

The atrium of the house looked much the same as the last time Nikias had seen it, but there was a cold, uninhabited kind of smell in the air. Most of the furniture had gone from the dining room and the office. Epaphras came toward them from one of the bedrooms.

"Kallion! I heard—everyone has been talking about your speech to the Civil Assembly yesterday. Your courage—you put me to shame. I don't know how to thank you."

The man looked utterly distraught, and at the same time almost exultant with relief—and probably more distraught with guilt over that. Nikias felt sorry for him.

"I came back to the city last night," he explained. "I couldn't let Satteia stay here without my support. I came to the house this morning, thinking I would face him. We were brothers, after all. I would"—He flapped a hand vaguely.—"make some fraternal gesture. Try to do my duty. I found the door open, and … I searched the house. It was deserted. It wasn't until I went into the menagerie—I had left instructions for the feeding of the animals, as you may recall, while we looked for buyers or a means to dispose of them. I thought to go in just to see whether they looked well cared for.

"That's where he was. I—I do think the animals may not have been fed as much as they might have been. At least one of them—I'm not sure which. At any rate, he was quite dead." He gestured toward the bedroom behind him. "We've just brought the body in, if you want to … er. I mean, considering what happened last time, you may wish … "

"Thank you, sir," said Kallion crisply. "I would like to take a look."

Nikias swallowed, grateful that Kallion stepped decisively away from him as he said this, not expecting Nikias to follow him into the room.

Satteia came through from the garden while Nikias was standing there awkwardly trying to think of something to say to Epaphras.

"Nikias!" She approached with open arms. She was

plainly not feeling any of the same conflicting emotions as her husband. "Shall we get to work right away rebuilding your stall? I will send for the carpenter, and you and Tiko can start on some of the basic repairs. Tell me what was stolen and destroyed, and I'll make a shopping list."

"I will leave you to it," said Epaphras. He leaned in to kiss his wife on the cheek—almost gingerly, as if he was being very, very careful after having come so close to losing her a second time.

"Did Kallion do it?" Satteia asked the moment her husband was out of earshot.

"Do what?"

She nodded toward the door of the room where her brother-in-law's body was laid out.

"No, I—I think a crocodile, or a tiger or something?"

"Yes, I know he was *killed* by an animal, but how did he get in there in the first place? Was that Kallion's doing? Did he arrange to have the animals not fed, and then … "

"No," said Nikias firmly. "He didn't. He would have told me if he had, and he hasn't told me, so he didn't."

Satteia looked convinced, but more than a little disappointed. Nikias saw Kallion standing outside the bedroom door, looking as if he had been there for some time. Of course it wouldn't have taken him long to look at his late master's body.

"I didn't," he said quietly, coming forward, his eyes on Nikias. "I could have—I had the perfect opportunity. I'd hired the men who were escorting him home—I could have paid them to knock him on the head and drag him into the menagerie. But I didn't."

"I know," said Nikias.

"I wouldn't have blamed you if you had," said Satteia wistfully.

"I would have blamed myself," said Kallion. "It's far too much something that he would have done himself. I have been afraid for too long of becoming evil because I was a tool in the service of evil. I don't think I'm afraid of that any more. I didn't kill him."

"Well," said Satteia, "someone did—and I don't mean the crocodile. That gate was locked from the outside when Epaphras got in this morning."

"It could have been any of dozens of people," Nikias said. If Satteia had not been the one telling them the story, his money would have been on her. "Think of all the people who must hate him, all the lives he ruined. Not to mention the pirates."

"Not to mention the pirates," Satteia said, nodding. "Well, I suppose we may never know. Though I wouldn't mind shaking whoever it was by the hand."

They said goodbye after that and went back out into the street. They paused to look at the cheap jewellery displayed in front of the stall that had taken the place of Pyke's Snacks.

"So he's dead?" Nikias prompted.

"Oh, extremely, yes."

In spite of everything, it would have felt wrong to say, "Hooray!" Nikias contented himself with an approving nod. He looked over the brightly coloured bracelets on display in the stall, then spotted something else on the shelf underneath.

"What did you do to celebrate when you were freed?" he asked suddenly, thinking he knew the answer.

"Nothing really. I went looking for an apartment, and I think I must have bought myself something for dinner—but it wasn't a celebration."

"Do you want one of these?" Nikias held up a dainty shell comb carved with flowers. "A gift to celebrate that you're *really* free now."

Kallion laughed, easily and beautifully. Nikias thought of how often he had watched him on just this street corner, drinking in the sight of him, not knowing anything but the beauty on the outside.

"I'll take it," he told the shopkeeper, fishing out a coin to pay.

They walked on up the street, away from the harbour, away from the house where Kallion had been born. Kallion stuck the shell comb into his hair, behind his ear.

# EPILOGUE

It was a bright, chill day at the beginning of the new year. The Tetrina Market was busy. Kallion looked up from the treatise on property law that he had been reading, as Nikias came around the counter and pulled up a stool to sit next to him.

"That's me done for the day," said Nikias. "Tiko and Itia can handle it from here. We can leave whenever you like."

"We've got it under control, sir," said Tiko from the other side of the counter.

Itia rolled her eyes. "You've really got to stop calling both of them 'sir.'"

"But Kallion's partly my boss now, too," Tiko protested.

Nikias's market stall had reopened a week ago. Kallion had wanted to help pay for the repairs, and Satteia had suggested making him a part owner. Kallion's heart had lept when Nikias's response had been a delighted, "Yes! What a good idea." It was just business, of course, but Kallion didn't think a man as practical as Nikias would agree to go into business with his lover if he didn't envision the affair lasting —well, maybe long enough that you wouldn't even call it an "affair" any more. He couldn't think of anything he wanted more.

Kallion rolled up his scroll and slipped it back into his satchel. "I'm ready," he said.

Nikias got up and reached for Kallion's hand, then pulled him in for a kiss. Hand in hand, they set off down the Tetrina Hill. They planned to meet Lysandros and the others at the Civil Palace, so there would be a big crowd, and Kallion savoured the walk there, choosing a route through less-trafficked streets to enjoy the quiet with Nikias.

"It's nice of everyone to come listen to me," he said as they went down a flight of stairs on a narrow back street.

"They're coming to cheer," said Nikias, grinning. "You're our star speaker, and this is your debut." He squeezed Kallion's hand. "I don't think I've said thank you yet. I know you're not doing this just because of me, but … "

Kallion stopped on the stairs. "I am doing it because of you, Niki. Not just because I'd do anything to make you happy, but because you've made me believe in this. You've made me want to use my skills for something worthwhile. You've made me brave enough to do it."

"Nobody needed to make you brave," said Nikias, but he looked pleased all the same.

They reached the agora and crossed toward the steps of the Civil Palace, crowded with citizens streaming in to attend the day's assembly. There was to be a discussion about a new aqueduct, which would probably take up the majority of the meeting, but there would always be time at the end for any citizen to stand up and speak on any topic. That was when Kallion would stand up and make his case against slavery, with his friends the radicals there to cheer him, and Nikias looking on with pride.

He wouldn't win any prizes, as he had at the oratory contests in his youth; he'd be lucky if anyone besides his friends and his lover paid any attention to him. That didn't matter. He would do it because it was right, because Nikias had given him that freedom, and he would use it.

"Remember you promised you'd make me octopus fritters when we get home," he said as they neared the Civil Palace steps.

"Of course. With extra sauce?"

"If you don't mind."

# JOIN THE CLUB

Join my *Fragments Club* list to get exclusive short stories and snippets!

Sign up at **ajdemas.com**

ALSO BY A.J. DEMAS

*Something Human*

*One Night in Boukos*

SWORD DANCE TRILOGY

*Sword Dance*

*Saffron Alley*

*Strong Wine*

WHEN IN PHEME

*Honey & Pepper*

# ACKNOWLEDGMENTS

*Honey & Pepper* is a book that had many false starts, and seemed for a while like it wouldn't make it into print at all. I'm grateful for all the help I had as I wrestled it into its final (and, I hope, satisfactory) shape. Thanks to Alexandra Bolintineanu and Lee Welch, my invaluable early readers, and to May Peterson, my wonderful editor. Thanks to Vic Gray for his gorgeous cover art. And warm thanks to everyone who expressed excitement about this book when I announced it on social media. You make me feel I'm doing something right!

# ABOUT THE AUTHOR

A.J. Demas is an ex-academic who formerly studied and taught medieval literature, and now writes romance set in a fictional world based on an entirely different era. She lives in Ontario, Canada, with her husband and cute daughter.

Find out about upcoming books and more here:
www.ajdemas.com

A.J. also publishes fantasy and historical fiction with a metaphysical twist under a different name (her real one). You can find those here: www.alicedegan.com